I0620291

Tales of the Unexpected

Russ Crossley

53RD STREET PUBLISHING

Tales of The Unexpected

Published by 53rd Street Publishing

Copyright 2012 Russ Crossley
All rights reserved
ISBN 978-1-927621-22-6
Cover art copyright © Rolffimages | Dreamstime.com
Logo image by:

Engraver | Dreamstime.com

This is a work of fiction. The persons and situations are
products of the authors imagination.

Dedication

Another for Rita who is my everything. I love you, sweetheart.

Table of Contents

Introduction

This is a collection of five stories I am exceptionally proud of because they all were written for workshops I attended taught by some of the best in the business. Kristine Katherine Rusch, Dean Wesley Smith, and Gardner Dozois were my teachers and my mentors for these workshops. They helped me to become a better writer and these stories represent my development under their tutelage for which I will be ever grateful.

I hope you enjoy these stories as much as I did writing them.

Russ Crossley
May 2013
Vancouver, Canada

In Search of the Perfect Cup

TREVOR WATKINS SAT PRONE in front of his Mac his fingers poised over the keyboard staring at the empty page. The gray cursor at the left side of the screen flashed intermittently as if to urge his long, narrow fingers to write. Something anything. Instead, it reminded him of his failure. His advance was nearing depletion and he had nothing to show for it. At least very little his publisher would appreciate.

The only thing interrupting the silence in his study came from his extra large tumbler of cola. It popped and fizzed to its own drummer oblivious to his frustration. The air was filled with the odor of sweet cola.

In conducting his research, Trevor had traveled to every country and city on Earth to find the perfect cup.

Not in the Paris café's or the Istanbul coffee houses or the London bistro's or the finest New York restaurants or even in the Mall of America. It seemed nowhere on God's blue Earth was the perfect cup to be found. He'd drunk so much swill that he was certain his blood had been replaced by black ooze. He was also sure he'd die of a coffee overdose before he finished. Either that or his editor would kill him. Of the two options open to him right now he preferred the latter. Wally would kill him for sure.

The editor of the largest publishing house in De Moines last e-mail had made Wally's intent plain. "Write or die" was as clear as anyone ever got about such things. And if he knew Wally Vesper as well as he did, he meant what he said.

You'd think after three successful coffee table books he should be able to write this one with ease. But he was stymied. And after all the project's he'd completed this one should be the easiest yet. It fulfilled his life-long dream. This was the reason he'd become a writer in the first place.

His hands dropped to his side then he leaned forward to rest his elbows on his pine work desk and eyed the screen as if it were his sworn enemy. Damn it, he'd interviewed thousands of people from every walk-of-life. Their eyes were lit by an inner passion when they told him where to find the perfect cup of the black elixir he called coffee. Busmen, waiters, construction workers, office workers, celebrities, coffee company executives, CEO's, dishwashers, they all said the same thing, "It was the best cup I ever tasted." Unfortunately, none measured up.

Maybe what he's sought for so long didn't exist? But how could that be? He'd had one, once. The most perfect cup he'd ever tasted had been only the once.

It was so long ago he could just barely recall that heavenly flavor. Even today, when he closed his eyes he swore he could still taste the aromatic flavor of it when the coffee mingled with cream and sugar and danced over his taste buds.

It was the time when he was a kid that his Mom had made him what was to be her last cup of coffee. At the tender age of thirteen she'd said he was finally old enough to have his first cup. She died in her sleep that night and her coffee recipe died with her. He'd never a tasted a cup like it since.

Trevor was a junkie. Hooked on the bean, his wife Charlotte told her friends at the local beauty parlor. He agreed with her. Why deny it? He was hopelessly addicted, but there were worse things in life.

When he'd approached Wally with the idea he thought the cynical publisher would never buy it. To his surprise, he loved the idea. Trevor recalled at the time how happy he'd been. He'd managed to blend his obsession with his work. What could be the more perfect match? Except, it hadn't worked out quite like he'd expected, had it?

With his eyes closed he hung his head; his long, gray-flecked hair covered his thin face. He buried his face in his hands shuddered then sat up and straightened himself in his chair. He needed to shake this mood off to get back to work. I'm a pro, he thought. Act like one.

His red-rimmed eyes focused on the screen in front of him. He wrinkled his nose. Ugh, he thought, I even smell bad to me. He paused to take a generous sip of the cola. The bubbles tickled his nose as the sweet soda went down his throat where it cooled his tongue and the inside of his mouth as it disappeared into his digestive tract.

Trevor pressed the button that would link him to the net. "Might as well," he muttered, "nothing else to do."

As usual the Internet opened up and took him to his own website. The flashy advertising of Starbucks and Coffee Express gyrated on the edges of his vision. The screen was now filled with the map that recorded his worldwide quest.

He glanced down and noted the tracker at the bottom right corner of the screen now showed over one hundred thousand hits. Not great but not bad either.

He consoled himself with the thought that if he ever managed to complete the book *some* of the people who took time to follow his travels might even buy it.

Something caught his eye. He stared in awe as his jaw hung loose. There. On the Oregon Coast… there's something different. He moved the cursor over the pacific coast and drilled down using the spyglass feature until he was at street level.

He focused on the area south of Lincoln City. Odd. There's a new dot on the map. Very tiny. Almost too small to see with the naked eye. It's a town he'd never seen before at that location. Between Nelscott and Taft. A place called Almost. Almost, Oregon?

A shiver of excitement ran through his body. Maybe it's a sign? He opened his favorites list and Googled the name. Almost Oregon. The list showed ten billion hits.

The first site listed was the town's website. He moved the cursor over the website and clicked it.

There wasn't much. Population six. Located on Highway 101 between Nelscott and Taft. Total area ten acres. One business. "Hmmm…Le Petite Café…The Little Café?" Trevor rubbed his gray streaked goatee absently with his long fingers as he studied the screen.

A sudden shiver ran up his spine as realization struck him like a wave from the cold pacific. "This might be it."

He swiveled his high-backed plush office chair and studied the dust-covered wall of travel books that lined the walls of his study. Stream of golden rays of sunlight cut through the dust bunnies that floated and danced in the stream of heaven like markers that poured in from the backyard. The window overlooked Charlotte's vegetable garden. The sweet, red tomatoes were due to be harvested later this afternoon when she returned from her appointment. But he knew he wouldn't be here to taste their burst of earthy flavor. No, he'd be on his way to Oregon.

He reached for the black portable com unit that always sat on his desk beside his computer interface. He punched the red on button and was met with silence. The battery was dead. He cursed softly. "When I'm focused I'm really focused. Damn," he muttered.

He hurried from the room and walked into the bright canary yellow kitchen to where the banana-shaped phone was attached to the wall. Charlotte had found this treasure so delightful at that charity auction last year. He hated the damn thing.

He picked the old fashioned receiver from its cradle and dialed the number of the airline he always used. A woman's voice answered after two rings.

"Welcome to Orbit Shuttle. Please note…" the automated message continued for several seconds until Trevor hit the back door code to bypass the automated menus.

Ever since the message service companies realized everyone knew to hit zero, or some other specific number to connect with a live person, they'd made it increasingly difficult to get through the menus. Trevor had befriended many of the shuttle company's employees in his travels and he was privy to the preferred customer code. Only the most frequent flyers were allowed this level of access. After over two thousand flights, in the past five years he'd become the most frequent flyer they'd ever had.

Ever since you'd been able to get from LA to Paris in two hours his hops and jumps around the world were becoming more the norm than the exception so he'd likely loose his preferred status soon enough.

One ring and someone picked up. "How may I help you?" said an over friendly male voice. He cringed inside but pressed on.

"Huh...Hi, this is Trevor Watkins. I'd like to book a shuttle flight to Lincoln City, Oregon please." He knew that when he said his name it would trigger the voice recognition software in the OSB System to bring his history file up on the screen sitting in front of the booking agent.

As usual it did. "Certainly, Mr. Watkins. And may I say sir this will be your two thousandth and thirteen flight with us so it will be charged at half the normal rate." Trevor allowed himself a smile. The OBS had been bribing him with half fares since flight one thousand and one, though he never got tired of the supposed discount. With security fees, state, federal and local taxes it didn't mean much anyway. But maybe with the savings Charlotte would be able to afford her pumpkin seeds for the fall pumpkin-growing contest she entered every year.

"Would you prefer coach or first class?"

"Coach as usual," Trevor said, knowing full well the agent could easily see that he'd flown coach on every flight he'd ever taken with the shuttle service.

The agent finished the booking then accepted his credit code for the purchase.

Trevor felt a sense of relief. At least there was enough to pay for the trip in the account. "Thank the God's of travel," he muttered as he fled the room to begin packing. A couple of day's worth of clothes and toiletries were all he'd need. And he'd leave a note for Charlotte. He was sure she'd understand. At least he hoped so.

***

When he entered the small shuttle terminal in Lincoln City from the wind-swept tarmac, he ran his fingers through his shoulder length dark pepper sprinkled hair. The ocean breezes often played havoc with his hair. He brushed it away from his eyes with one hand all the while maintaining his iron grip with the other on his worn and faded leather briefcase. It was a family heirloom left to him by his father.

He headed for the baggage pickup in the small terminal A bored red cap stood leaning on his anti-grav luggage trolley waiting for someone to approach who needed help. In the front of the terminal was where the hover cars and sky buses waited to take arriving passengers to the string of seaside hotels and resorts that dotted this section of the Oregon coast.

Gambling, beachcombing, and partying were the sports of interest to anyone who usually visited this part of the world. None of these pursuits held any interest for Trevor.

He stood by the baggage drop and tapped one cowboy booted foot to mark his impatience while his sunglasses that shielded eyes allowed him to study his fellow passengers. It was a hobby of his. A way to collect characters for the great American novel he planned to write someday.

A steel gray haired man, on the high side of sixty, dressed in an impeccable navy pin striped suit, white shirt and red power tie, stood patiently watching the numbers of the arriving shuttles as they flashed on the baggage drop screen. Their luggage would materialize shortly once it was put through the reconfigure device used by the major carriers these days. Gone were the days when luggage consumed so much take off weight. Their luggage was reduced in weight by molecular reconfiguration to lighter than air materials. Once they arrived at their destination, the luggage was reconfigured into its original form. Worked like a charm every time.

Trevor spotted a young couple who looked to be on their honeymoon snuggling and holding hands. They gazed longingly into each other's eyes.

Trevor vividly recalled the times he and Charlotte had been like that. He recalled her perfume in his nostrils as he'd nuzzled her neck, and the softness of her lips as he kissed them.

He shook off the memories before they threatened to overwhelm him. His one regret was not being with Charlotte much over the last five years. It was hard on them both to be apart so much. If it weren't for the thrill of the chase, he'd have abandoned the project long ago.

Finally, the ground crew arrived with the glass tube that contained everyone's luggage. The two workers, one man the other a woman, gingerly placed the glass tube, that reminded Trevor of Mr. Billings beakers in his tenth grade biology class, on the platform. Within seconds, there was an eruption of light as a burst of energy was released. After the flash faded, and the spots before Trevor's eyes cleared, the luggage that belonged to shuttle flight thirteen passengers stood in three neat rows ready to go.

Trevor spotted his small, maroon colored hard sided over night case. Charlotte said it looked like a woman's makeup bag, an observation he didn't appreciate.

He picked up his bag then looked for the rental car company he'd booked before leaving home.

It was the same one he'd used many times before.

After the crowd of passengers had somewhat dissipated, he finally saw the rental agency booth against the far wall near the exit doors. There was no one behind the desk.

He walked over then bent down to place his bag and briefcase on the polished marble floor next to him. He straightened to find the clerk's smiling features watching him. Behind the counter was a young blond woman with one of those "how can I help you" smiles on her high cheek-boned face. Her blue eyes sparkled in the low light of the terminal. The perfect service industry employee, thought Trevor.

He smiled briefly in return then said, "I believe you have a reservation under the name, Watkins?"

"The woman's eyes traveled over her screen set below the counter, aligned so she was the only one who could see it. She nodded. "Yes, sir. Two days is it?"

"Yes, that's right."

She held out a small pad upon which he pressed the thumb of his right hand. This would verify his identity and debit his credit account for the charges. He waited while the system ran through its checks.

He felt a sense of unease as the woman's eyes flitted over the screen then up at him.

Her smile widened as the checks came back positive.

There was an audible click. The rental system computer had created the starter card encoded with his information and access permission. The card and his thumbprint would be needed to start the car. Without both pieces of information the vehicle disabler would come on, the doors would lock, and a signal would be sent to the police to investigate.

He thanked the young woman, (whose plastic nametag said she was Pam) then turned and left the terminal. The hover cars for rent were lined in a neat row near the one story building. He walked down the line of shiny new vehicles until he came to the number indicated on the starter card. It was one of the perks of traveling to drive the newer models. His car at home was a fifty-seven whose best years were far in the past.

The hover car selected for him was a canary yellow two-door coupe. Kinda sporty, he thought. Even so, it would be underpowered so no fancy racing about this trip.

He placed his over night bag in the trunk, but decided to keep his briefcase in the front seat with him on the passenger seat. He wasn't about to take any chances losing his baby.

He started the engine by inserting the card in the slot in the dashboard. It came to life purring as contentedly as a satisfied kitten. He felt the surge of power run through the little compact. He engaged the flight controls with a brief touch of the steering column and the car lifted gently off the ground. The autopilot engaged and he eased back in the seat getting comfortable as the seat molded itself to conformed to his lanky writer's body

Soon he was clear of the shuttle port parking lot headed south on the 101. He idly studied the massive homes and resorts that lined the expressway as they crawled forward in the stream of traffic. The car would handle the traffic without his intervention, which was considerable on this stretch of highway at this time of year. It was spring and the snowbirds were heading south in droves.

He pressed the button for the satellite tracking system and the face of the dashboard rolled up to reveal a small screen. It came on and showed him where he was in relation to his destination. He'd already pre-entered his destination when he booked the car so the on-board computer would know the way.

He felt a surge of excitement as he noted that they were within thirty minutes of arrival.

The traffic ahead was slow so the four kilometers would take an eternity. He pushed the negative thoughts away as he realized he might finally be coming to the end of his quest.

***

He glided past the strip mall twice as the car went back and forth over the same stretch of highway. The autopilot bleated at him every time he passed the spot just before the bridge that separated Nelscott from Taft. He puzzled over this.

How could the computer be telling him he'd missed his destination when it didn't appear to exist at all? Finally, he'd had enough. There was a gift shop on the Nelscott side of the bridge. He took control of the hover controls and steered the car into the parking lot.

He got out and went inside. A teenage looking boy, probably no more than eighteen, stood behind the waist-high laminated counter of the Nelscott Gift Emporium and Book Shop as he walked in. Trevor preferred to ask directions in stores that sold books. It seemed to him that readers were a tight community and could more easily relate to other readers. And besides writers were like Gods to these people.

Or so he'd experienced in the past when he'd explained he was a writer conducting research. They'd fall all over themselves to help him.

He strolled to the counter with a slight smile on his narrow features. The bespectacled teenager with short brown hair and watery hazel eyes glanced up when he heard the door open. His expression was bland and he didn't show any sign of a reaction to Trevor's easy charm. Am I losing my touch? he thought.

"Hi, I'm lost. I was wondering if you could give me directions."

The teen shrugged his broad shoulders. Trevor could see the teenager was built like a football player, with an expansive chest and wide shoulders underneath his forest green sweatshirt that said Auburn across the front in gold lettering.

"Yeah, sure."

"Great. I'm looking for Almost. Do you know where it is?"

The teenage shrugged. "Nope. Sorry. Never heard of it. I'm just here for the summer. You'll have to talk to one of the locals."

Trevor nodded and gave the teen a brief smile. "Is there someone else here that might know?"

"Let me check."

The teenager left Trevor standing at the counter as he disappeared through an arch behind him guarded by a bead curtain where the storeroom must be.

Trevor stood his booted foot tapping out the latest Broadway musical he'd heard over the sound system on the shuttle until, after several moments, the young man reappeared followed by an older woman.

She wore old-fashioned granny glasses, and her straight gray hair was pulled into a ponytail. Her craggy features broke into a sparkling white smile when she saw him standing there. She wore khaki shorts, brown sandals and a smoke gray sleeveless shirt. A few beads of perspiration dotted her creased forehead.

She held out one weathered hand. "Trevor Watkins isn't it?" she said in a surprisingly youngish sounding voice.

"Huh…yes. Do I know you?" He took her hand in his. Her grip was firm and surprisingly warm. She looked just this side of eighty.

She shook her head. "Oh, no, but I know who you are from your picture on the jackets of your books. I never forget a face." She appeared thoughtful for a brief second. "I especially enjoyed the one about the antique New England rocking chairs. Fascinating, truly fascinating."

He released her hand and said, "I'm flattered indeed, madam. And impressed you even bothered to read that one."

She waved away his objections then a look of concern wrinkled her brow. "Oh my, I should have introduced myself. Elizabeth Salmon." She paused to place one arm around the waist of the young man, "And this young fella is my nephew, Peter."

The teenager smiled through pursed lips. He was obviously uncomfortable with his Aunts open display of affection.

"He's my sister's boy, on hiatus from college for the summer. I'm paying him a small salary to help him out, and keep him out of trouble." Peter blushed and turned away to disappear into the back room.

"So, Peter tells me you're looking for Almost." She placed her hands on her narrow hips and eyed him as if to gauge his reaction.

Trevor nodded. He liked this woman already and he'd only just met her. "Yes, do you know where I might find it?' She nodded then with one hand rubbed her chin. "Yes I do, Mr. Watkins....I just don't know if that's a place you really want to go."

"Why not? And please call me Trevor."

The air was suddenly filled with mystery. Trevor felt the ache of excitement grow in his belly. He knew it! He'd been right. He didn't know how but this trip was different than all the others. He sensed the end of his travels were near, very near.

She nodded and the look in her eye told him she'd reached a decision. "Okay, Trevor. I'll take you," she said with a sly grin. She glanced behind her at the archway leading to the storeroom. "Peter, you watch the store. I'll be back in a while."

"Okay, Auntie Betty." The echo of Peter's reply was followed by an audible grunt that marked physical labor. The boy was hard at work.

Betty smiled warmly then came around the counter that separated them to link one arm under Trevor's. "Where's your car?" she said in a musical lilt.

They walked to the parking lot then got into the rental hover car. Betty leaned over, then using the keypad attached to the internal guidance computer, as she keyed in the coordinates.

She smiled briefly and nodded as Trevor touched the flight controls as before and they lifted off. The engine purred softly in his ears and Betty's slight odor of jasmine now filled the car. He reveled in the smell of it.

The scent reminded him of Charlotte's flower garden.

The car hovered at the entrance to the expressway as it waited for an opening in the traffic. Finally both lanes were clear and the car accelerated pressing them both back in the conform seats, the servomotors straining audibly to keep them as comfortable as possible. To Trevor's surprise, they had crossed the highway to the other side. There was an ancient gravel turn off. A left over from the days when wheeled vehicles ruled the highways and byways.

The car floated across the wide expanse of gravel until he saw an opening in the forest greenery that was invisible from the main road. To his surprise it was a road, of sorts. Not much of one, really. To be honest it looked more like an ancient wagon path than a road. Branches from low hanging trees crowded the narrow road as the car proceeded down the well-traveled path. Arm like branches of pines and oaks scrapped over the polished surface of the car. Trevor cringed each time heavy coarse needles ran down the roof and sides of the expensive car. He was certain he'd lose his insurance deductible.

Betty seeing his discomfort chuckled lightly. "Don't worry, Trevor. You'll never see a mark." Somehow, he doubted her.

Finally, after ten minutes they were approaching a clearing. An ancient wooden single story building with peeling paint, and a single door with a screen door that hung limply off its hinges came into view. Upon seeing it, Trevor began to doubt the old woman. Maybe she had screw loose.

"Here we are," she said brightly, as the hover car came to a halt next to the dilapidated structure then dropped gently to the grass covered meadow that surrounded the time–worn building.

"Where is here?" Trevor said as he studied the sad looking structure intently. It looked as if it were a hundred years old at least or maybe older. It's a wonder it hadn't collapsed long ago. The wood was gray and weathered and the little chips of sky blue paint that were left were likely the only thing holding it together.

"Trevor Watkins, may I present Le Petite Café!" She burst into a wide smile as she flung the passenger door open and stepped out onto the wind bent grass. He watched her pause to fill her lungs with a deep breath of air.

For several seconds Trevor considered closing the doors and fleeing but he actually liked this old woman so he decided he better join in her fantasy.

He opened his door and was hit with the smells of the forest.

The grass and trees ejected such a base cornucopia of nature at him that he felt suddenly at one with his surroundings. It was like those times when he was a kid and his father had taken him hiking in the hills surrounding their home in Lake Wenatchee.

He followed her as she headed for the broken down shack. Reluctantly he walked after her shaking his head in sadness. She was a mad old woman. He should have known better after seeing the reactions of her nephew. If the young man were really her nephew and if his name was actually Peter, which he doubted.

At the door, she waited for him, then as he approached, she opened it with flourish and stepped inside. It looked dark inside.

He squinted then stepped through. He blinked once then found himself standing inside a brightly lit room that for all the world looked like those old-fashioned roadside diners he'd seen in period movies.

A man with a slate gray goatee, wearing a black western hat with a colorful band of gold and silver round the center was busy wiping the shiny apple red lunch counter with a white cloth as they came in. The smell of coffee and fresh baked apple pie permeated the room. There was a row of polished steel stools with ruby-colored cushions atop them, as if they were cherry Popsicles.

22

The row of empty stools was broken by a lone figure who sat on the one farthest from the door.

The man wiping the counter glanced up from his work as they entered and smiled warmly. "Hey, Betty, long time no see."

"Hey yourself Hardee," Betty said nodding toward Trevor, "Brought a guest with me."

"Yeah I can see that. We've been expecting him."

Trevor's eyes went wide as Betty guided him to the counter where they each took a seat beside each other.

"So where you been?" said Hardee gazing at Betty.

"My sister's boy is with me this summer and I have to keep on eye on him. You know what these teenagers can be like."

Hardee's indigo eyes sparkled and he laughed lightly. "Yeah, I know what you mean."

"What did you mean?" blurted Trevor when he'd regained sufficient composure.

The figure at the end of counter spoke up interrupting Hardee before he could reply. "He means how did you know he was comin'?"

Trevor glanced toward this new voice, a man's voice.

At the end of the lunch counter sat a man, who from the look of him had to be seven feet in height, if he was an inch. His voice contained an odd echoing quality to it as if he were speaking from the bottom of a well. His sleeveless arms were covered in tattoos that ran from his bare shoulders to his wrists. He was tanned like someone who'd worked outdoors all his life. Dark jet-black curls stuck out from beneath the brim of an Australian bush hunter's hat two sizes too small for his huge head. His dark eyes seemed to bore into Trevor sending a shiver of dread through him.

"Oh knock off the drama will ya, Milt," said Hardee with a laugh. "Don't worry about him." Hardee waived his hand at Milt who went back to sipping from a white china coffee cup. The giant's wide grin made Trevor feel even more ill at ease.

The door that Trevor assumed led to the kitchen suddenly was thrown open and a large purple slug with wings floated through. A white paper chef's hat sat perched atop what must be the head, as it was the end facing forward as it <u>flew</u>. Web-like wings stuck out from its body two feet to either side. Trevor raised one trembling index finger at the being unable to utter a single sound. His jaw hung open as he stared at the slug thing. He was frozen to his seat.

Hardee rolled his eyes. "Wally, didn't I tell you to stay in the back until I told the lad a little more about us?"

The slug thing, somehow dubbed Wally, shrugged and lifted on the air stirred by its wings floated to the row of soda dispensers against the roughed pine wall. An arm appeared from its purple gelatin like body. It seemed to grow from its body before his eyes. It used this newly created arm to grasp a drink glass it retrieved from under the counter. Another arm appeared and it drew itself a glass of cola. "Sorry, H. I was getting' thirsty. It's friggin' hot back there ya know." Its voice was normal, sort of sounded human with a slight Texas drawl.

Wally must be from Texas, thought Trevor.

The purple slug paused to hover in front of him. Trevor felt the air from the action of its wings waft over him. All he could smell was the odor of the cola.

"Sorry. Hope you're havin' a nice day," said Wally. The sincerity in its voice was unmistakable.

"Huh…sure no problem…"

Wally the flying purple slug left them alone once again when he disappeared through the door he'd come in by.

"Where the hell am I," said Trevor gazing at Hardee then turning his attention to Betty who shrugged, a small knowing smile on her lips.

"Now, Trevor my boy…" began Hardee.

Trevor gave the diner owner a warning look then focused his attention on the old woman. Her smile disappeared and her eyes dropped to the counter. After a momentary pause she gazed hard into his eyes. Hers were now were tinged with pain.

"Trevor, I know this will be very hard to understand, but your mother wasn't of this world. She was from outside. Another place. Another dimension." She paused and pointed at the door where Wally had disappeared only seconds before. "That's where Wally and all of us here came from. That's the place Elizabeth came from." She waved one hand around then continued. "This place, this diner is our refuge. A place where we come to get away from the world you've always known as home. A place where, as the kids are so find of saying, 'We can let our hair down'." She gazed at him her eyes watery.

"Do you understand?"

Trevor shook his head. "No, not really…" But from somewhere deep inside he realized he did know what they were talking about. He'd been drawn here. This was home.

Hardee smiled "We know why you're here, Trevor my boy. You're here to find the perfect cup of coffee, of course."

Trevor looked at the coffee shop man through narrowed eyes. How did he know that? He'd not said anything to Betty or anyone else about why he was coming here. He'd not even taken the time to leave that note for Charlotte. No one knew why he was here. No one except his loyal followers…yes that had to be it.

"You've been to my website?"

"Sorry, old fella we don't have one of those 'puters round here." As if to emphasize his point Hardee's eyes moved around the room. Betty snickered behind her hand, her gray eyes dancing with amusement.

Now Trevor was really bewildered. "Well, then how did you know I was coming?"

Hardee smiled warmly, moved to the wall behind him, and retrieved a white china cup like the one Milt was sipping from, and a matching saucer. He hadn't noticed it there before but Trevor realized he was looking at the largest collection of glass tubing this side of the bio-lab at MIT. The tubing ran in loops and curves like a fragile nest of clear wires. At one end sat an oval shaped bowl that contained boiling water.

Then bubbling water traveled through the glass tubes until it ended at a pile of dark Earthen looking powder. From here it was pushed upward (by what means he had no idea, as it seemed to defy gravity) until it connected to a tube filled with the now darkened liquid ending at a spout with a tap. Hardee eyes smirked at Trevor as he moved to the spout. He opened the tap after placing the cup and saucer underneath and there was the sound of running water until the cup was filled to the brim. Hardee then came back to place the cup in front of Trevor with a click of china on arborite.

"This is how. And why."

Trevor hesitated with his confused gaze fixed on the black steaming liquid that filled the cup to the brim. There was a steel creamer in front of him and a bowl of snow-white sugar next to it. He picked up a metal spoon and placed one heaping spoon of sugar in the cup then a dollop of cream form the creamer. He was certain he'd regret this, but he took the cup in both hands and brought it to his lips.

The heavenly aroma that assaulted him quickly overwhelmed his senses. A flood of memories filled his mind as the mixture of odors permeated his every bodily orifice. He pictured his sweet mother on that day all those years ago. Her toothpaste smile, her hazel eyes, her healthful flushed cheeks....

He stopped the cup in mid-air and felt a rush of grief wash over him.

He replaced the cup on the saucer as tears welled in his eyes. "Why?" he managed to croak before his voice choked in his throat.

"It's alright, Trevor," said Betty softly taking his hand in hers.

Trevor turned to look at her, tears blinding her features to him as the salty trails of moisture began run in rivulets down his cheeks.

"There, there," she cooed. He moved toward her and buried his face in her shoulder. She cupped his head gently and murmured words of encouragement.

Finally, the feeling passed and Trevor managed to sit up. He again the raised the cup to his lips and this time successfully swallowed some. It tasted ordinary. Bitter. Not at all what he'd expected. He replaced the cup once more.

"She was one of us," said Hardee.

"One of what?" said Trevor.

"I think you know," said Betty taking both of his hands in hers and gazing deep into his eyes. He nodded. Of course, he knew. He'd always known.

***

Trevor sat perched on the edge of his chair pounding furiously at his keyboard when he heard Charlotte walk in. The words seemed to flow from his fingers to the screen as if he were taking dictation.

He swiveled his office chair to face his wife a wide grin pasted to his face as she entered. She reeked of perm solution, which would normally bother him, but instead it was the most pleasant smell on the planet.

"How's the book coming?" she said.

"Almost finished."

She chuckled. "Wonderful. What do you want to do to celebrate?"

"How about a holiday?"

"What a great idea! Where do you want to go?"

"How about the Oregon coast?"

"Why there?"

Trevor shrugged. "Oh, I don't know. Maybe it's because Mom loved the place. And they do have the best coffee in the universe."

"Okay." Charlotte shrugged then turned and left the room closing the door behind her.

He smiled to himself. Yeah, the coffee may be instant but the place was magic.

T.I.N. MEN

THE U.S. ARMY ISSUED ergonomic chair beneath Technical Sergeant Will Arnett trembled. Uncertain what was happening, Will's eyes drifted to the half empty glass of coke he'd earlier placed on the cup holder recessed into the consol next to his elbow.

Or was it half full? He'd always hated pop psychology, and was far too practical for such limited cerebral arguments. In his civilian life he had a PhD in software engineering and he programmed software. Everything in the world was either a one or a zero, nothing more.

He watched the sweet brown liquid splash up along the sides of the glass then his hazel eyes flitted sharply back to the three screens recessed into the console in front of him. The deck shuddered again, only more violently this time.

The screens provided him a 360 degree view of the dry, cactus and scrub brush dotted Arizona landscape surrounding the Styker reconnaissance vehicle.

He swallowed hard and his eyes went wide as an unbelievable site appeared on the center screen. He would later say he'd seen as a silver and gray robot that the onboard sensors said was over sixty feet in height suddenly appear out of the gloom of first light. It's body was human shaped with a wide chest and a head that swiveled as it scanned the desert. It moved in giant footsteps each the length of a Cadillac. It was headed westerly ninety degrees from his position.

It was barely past sunrise and the blue velvet sky glowed orange, yellow, and red as the sun's tendrils chased away the night. Since the desert can play tricks on you at sunrise Will blinked a few times, but the robot didn't vanish. This was impossible. I must be dreaming. If it were real though it would sure be fascinating.

Will had been on watch all night in the Styker on a military exercise in this patch of barren desert. As day approached he'd begun to wonder who he'd pissed off to rate this duty. Fortunately the Styker was a nuclear, biological, chemical reconnaissance vehicle, or NBCRV.

This meant if they were properly equipped (which they were not) the five person crew could survive inside this tin can for up to two weeks.

Will's heart beat hard in his chest and he fought the urge to bolt from his chair as the massive robot on the screen took a step closer. The vehicle bounced on its undercarriage.

With trembling fingers, Will pulled down the mouth mike attached to his armored helmet he'd pushed out of his way. He needed to contact Lieutenant Sims in the command cab up front. The mike was voice activated, "Huh, sir."

No response.

"Sir! Lieutenant!"

The ground shook as the robot increased it's pace. It occurred to Will the Styker might not withstand being crushed underfoot by this mechanical monster. He didn't know why he thought this, but this robot's appearance had created an unusual situation after all.

"Yeah," came the sleepy reply of the Lieutenant who was sitting in the driver compartment forward of the surveillance control center. There was a hatch between the control center and the drivers compartment which the LT kept locked when he was up front with the driver.

The colonel had sent them out with himself, the lieutenant, and a rookie private named Pike as driver, on what he called a training mission. The mission objective was to simulate the loss of crew members to test how resourceful they could be with only three remaining crew versus a normal compliment.

Will swallowed hard when he recalled they didn't even have .50 cal ammunition for the M2 machine gun.

"What is it, grunt?" came the annoyed reply.

Will cringed. Sims was regular Army. He was reserves so Sims rode him pretty hard when ever the opportunity presented itself. "Sir, there's a giant robot coming straight at us. Sir." He added the second sir, because he knew how ludicrous what he'd just said sounded.

He watched the robot stop then the dark pupiless eyes set in the human shaped head swiveled and seemingly look right at him through the video screen. The remaining moisture in his mouth evaporated.

"A robot?" Sims grunted. "You bin watching cartoons back there?"

"Huh, no, sir. Believe me it's real. Turn on the external lights. Sir."

"OK, grunt, but if you've woken me for nothin' I'm gonna kick your ass all the way back ta base."

Will heard the sound of a toggle switch through his head set.

"What the...." Sims voice trembled. "Pike! Wake up! Get us the hell outta here, we —"

Sims voice was cut off when every screen went dark and the familiar hum of the air exchange died. Will held his breath as he waited for the emergency generator to kick in, but nothing happened. They were dead in the water. Will sat in darkness. His breathing became shallow. The air already seemed stuffy and a few degrees warmer. A trickle of sweat ran down his left cheek and back.

This is impossible. The M1135 NBC Reconnaissance Vehicle, or Styker, was designed to be impervious to Electro Magnetic Pulse attack. The exterior hull was constructed from a titanium alloy. Sloped armor would deflect an EMP attack. The interior walls were lined with a rubber liner to absorb electricity. The hull was also shielded from radiation by sealed lead paint, and the vehicle had its own internal air and recycling filtration system so a gas attack would be useless.

They were as safe as anyone on earth from non-conventional attack could be.

Unfortunately, since the armor plating on the sides was thin, only 14 millimeters thick, conventional weapons, or a giant robot foot, could easily destroy them.

Will said a silent prayer. He was about to die.

The vehicle around him trembled then he winced at he awful screech of metal on metal. He was gripped by a feeling of weightlessness. The vehicle around him shuddered as it was lifted into the air. His stomach muscles tighten as nausea enveloped him.

Will reached out to grip the edge of the consol and held on as tightly as he was able. Whatever was happening was causing his lean frame to alternate between straining against the restraining strap across his chest, he'd been insightful enough to have on, and become weightless as if her were floating in a swimming pool.

Fear welled from his belly as he realized the robot must have picked up the Styker and was carrying it as if it were a child's toy. But where were they going?

***

After half an hour the swaying stopped and the vehicle bounced once more as it was placed on the ground.

Will who's heart still pounded rapidly in his chest, and was frozen in his chair his sweaty fingers in a death grip on the chair arms. They'd stopped moving. Will let out a breath he'd been holding. He didn't much care where on terra firma he was, just that the shaking had stopped. He let out a breath he'd been holding and wiped his brow with the sleeve of his uniform jumper.

So far the robot hadn't threatened them.

"You in the M1135," said a booming mechanical voice over his headset. "Come out or we will destroy you."

Okay, that sounded like a threat. But who was we?

In the last thirty minutes, Will had mapped out a plan of action in his head. The robot was tall, it's hands were probably twenty feet or more from the ground. If he got out and took off running he would run between its legs before it could react. He'd find a hiding place the where robot was too large to follow until he could find a radio or a telephone to call the base. What are my options?

The Styker didn't have any surface-to-robot missiles, hand grenades, or as much as firecracker for that matter, so he couldn't fight the thing. Styker vehicles never carry weapons.

And he couldn't surrender that would be cowardice in the face of the enemy, and if he survived the idea of spending time at Leavenworth prison cell made him the ultimate coward. The army really hated the word surrender. His superiors would not be amused.

No. All he could do was run for his life. To fight another day of course. It was a strategic retreat.

Somehow he didn't think a giant robot that seized U.S. Army property was a friendly so it had to be fought. America was the land of shoot first ask questions later. That much was clear. But he didn't think of himself as the man for the job. I'm a software engineer, not a warrior.

The real questions were, how did a giant robot get into the middle of the Arizona desert, and why was it here?

He rose on unsteady legs from the chair and took in a deep breath to try and settle down his nerves. His cheeks puffed out as he released his breath stuttering gasps. He wiped the sweat from his brow with the back of his hand.

The emergency escape hatch was at the rear of the control center. He stumbled across the deck his hands reaching out in front of him. Quickly his finger tips made contact with the smooth walls of the vehicle.

He managed to make his way to where he recalled the hatch was located without falling over one of the chairs at the workstations. He yelped as the toe of his right boot struck the hatch. He winced and swallowed hard.

Geez, that hurts.

The pain gradually subsided until finally he knelt down and felt for the hatch release. He found it and pulled the handle toward him. The hatch swung in and the control center was suddenly awash in blinding light. He closed his eyes tightly and waited for his eyes to adjust.

Holding one hand up to shield his eyes he blinked but managed to squeeze out the hatch without falling. At least I can keep some of my dignity.

So far his escape plan hadn't worked so well. He couldn't run blindly unable to see where he was headed could he?

"Stay right where you are, Sergeant." The voice was deep but mechanical.

Knowing a threat when he heard one Will froze and waited. He suspected if it meant to kill him he would already be dead.

His eyesight gradually began to clear, sufficiently so he could make out fuzzy shapes. One he expected the other he did not.

The forbidding very tall, very wide shape had to be the robot. Beside the large blob of fuzz was a smaller more human sized shape. And it had curves. Female curves.

What the...? Where am I?

"You ok, sergeant?" said the woman.

Will blinked and the woman came into sharper focus. She was dressed in blue jeans, sneakers, and wore a bright orange tee shirt with the words MR. FUZZ emblazoned across her full breasts.

"Name's Arnett. Will Arnett. Technical Sergeant United States Army. Serial number —"

She laughed cutting him off in his name-rank-and-serial-number spiel. He had never been given an order to only provide these details, but he'd seen enough movies to know this was the procedure when captured by the enemy.

At least they seemed like an enemy. He eyed the shapely woman with her laughing blue eyes, dimple in her right cheek, and smirk on her lips. Funny thing was she wasn't acting like an enemy.

"Huh, sorry," he said. "That was about as stupid as I feel right now." Suddenly as if from nowhere anger welled up from the pit of his stomach.

She chuckled. He detected the scent of lemons coming from her direction.

"I think it was kind of cute actually."

"I have a question for you," Will said.

She smiled and held up a tablet reader she'd been holding in her left hand. "Everything you need to know is on here. If you follow me we'll get some breakfast while you read."

Will frowned. She was avoiding the obvious and he was getting pissed off. "OK, I'll agree but you have to tell me your name first."

She chuckled and shook her head. "I'm sorry. We don't get many visitors so my social skills are somewhat lacking. My name's Holly Hope. I'm a scientist, like you."

***

The walked down the well lit corridor toward what appeared to be elevator doors at more than twenty feet away. Where am I?

"Are we underground?" he asked.

Holly nodded. "Oh, yes, about a mile down actually."

Will let go with a soft whistle. Good thing I'm not claustrophobic.

What was lightning the corridor wasn't obvious, but he suspected the ceiling was painted with a florescent paint backlit by low wattage light tubes. This told him they were trying to conserve power. Interesting. He wondered if they could generate enough power to fuel a sixty foot tall robot why they needed to conserve power. He mentally field the information away.

"So, Holly, where are my lieutenant, and the driver?" So far, Holly had been relaxed and wore an easy smile on her lips. She wasn't armed as far as he could tell, but she had made him curious, especially when she revealed she was had a PhD in biotechnology. And somehow she knew he was had a PhD in software engineering.

He frowned. How does she know so much about me? He looked at her walking beside him. She was sure cute, and apparently smart. He liked those qualities in a woman.

"Randall will drop them back on the spot in the desert where he picked you up," she said as casually as if she'd just made a run to the corner store for a candy bar. "No need to worry about them. They'll be fine."

He looked at her. "Who's Randall?"

She chuckled. Is everything I say funny? I know I'm not funny.

"Sorry. The robot who brought you here. His name's Randall." She used one index finger to make a twirling motion next to her head. "I can be so spiny sometimes. I forget you haven't been here before. Randall is one of our 'bots."

Will swallowed and his stomach tightened. "One?"

"Yeah. I mean, yes." They had reached the elevator doors. Affixed to the wall next to the doors was a black proximity reader. It had ridges in it's surface but was otherwise devoid of any markings.

Holly pulled a white plastic card about the size of a credit card from her right pocket and swiped it over the prox reader. The elevators doors parted. She stuffed the card back in her pocket then her eyes locked on his.

"You ready?"

Will swallowed hard. "For what?"

The sides of her mouth curled slightly but her eyes became flat. The humor had left her as if the air in a balloon was being released slowly. It unnerved him.

"To see the most incredible things you have ever seen."

Will wondered what she meant, but the scientist in him boiled to the surface.

He had to know where that robot came from and where he was and who was behind this. Holly didn't have the specialty to build the robot. Once she told him about her specialty which was chemical engineering, he knew there had to have been others involved.

A knot of excitement shredded the fear had felt earlier. Like Mulder and Scully he had to know the truth.

"Yes, Holly, I am ready."

Her features changed back to the friendly grin and her eyes sparkled as they had before. "Great. You must meet, Dr. Good."

Will nodded.

They entered the elevator and the doors closed behind them. Holly used the card to swipe over another proximity card reader. There were no buttons and no floor numbers. The walls were bare except for the card reader.

There was a slight sensation of movement that was barely detectable. Will wondered if they were moving at all.

Holly became his tour guide. "We'll be traveling to the underground living quarters and research facilities twenty stories underground. The quarters house up to twenty-seven research scientists.

We have several specialists who are experts in their fields; chemistry, biology, propulsion, exobiology, bioelectronics, biomechanics, and engineers in the fields of aerospace, and chemical engineering. We also have several PhD's who worked at JPL on interplanetary exploration."

"Is there a brochure?" Will muttered.

Holly looked at him with one eyebrow raised and laughed. "I like you already. You're funny."

The elevator stopped. The doors slid open. Will's jaw dropped. The vast expanse reminded him of his favorite '50's science fiction movie, Forbidden Planet.

The area was vast with diamond shaped corridors leading off a central common area teaming with people, some riding four wheeled electric trucks and some wearing white lab coasts carrying tablets and what looked like cell phones though he suspected they weren't cell phones. This far underground the most powerful cell on the commercial market wouldn't be able to get a signal.

The floors were polished black rock with veins of color running through it. And there were quite a number of robots. Not as big as the one that had snatched him, they were six feet tall and shiny silver in color.

They had no eyes but must have sensors because they moved agley among the humans, who took no interest in them. It was as if robots were normal.

I'm clearly not in Kansas anymore. Or Arizona to be exact.

"I told you." Holly exited the elevator.

Will regained his composure and chased after her as she led him across the vast central hub. She was right. This was incredible. He caught up with her as she continued her tour guide spiel. She explained that the corridors led to the laboratories, the recreation area, a cafeteria and the living quarters. "We're going to the directors office first. Dr. Good is anxious to meet you."

Will noticed above each corridor was a large illuminated capital letter. They were about to enter corridor D. "Who is this, Dr. Good?"

"He's the director of the project. He has four PhD's, and has been director of the project since it started in 1967."

"Oh, really?" Will refrained from rolling his eyes. Good was an old man, probably with old man ideas. A robot walked past them in the corridor. Well, maybe not that old.

They passed several men and women who nodded to Holly as they went by but seemed to ignore him. They seemed a cold, unfriendly bunch.

He wondered now why he was here.

Finally they arrived outside a door recessed into the side of the corridor. There was no door handle or lock. Beside it was another prox card reader. Holly glanced at him and offered a closed mouth smile. She swiped her card over the reader and the door slid open and into the doorframe.

Beyond the entrance was a well lit office with a glass desk (he recognized it was made of plexi-glass not real glass. His old prof used to have one just like it). The desk had a flat screen in one corner and a pen set in a wooden holder near the front edge of the desk. The two items could not be more dissimilar. The old clashed with the new.

Two red leather chairs sat in front of the desk. Against one wall to his right was a matching red leather sofa. Hung on the wall over the sofa was a painting of the Saturn V rocket in flight.

They entered the office together with Holly slightly ahead as the lead.

Sitting behind the desk sipping a dark liquid from glass was a small man. He looked about the size of a ten year old, only the steel gray hair that ringed his bald spot, and the wrinkles around the intense green eyes told Will he was much older than he at first appeared.

"Sit down, Sergeant," the man said, his tone gentle but firm. Will sat down burying his hands in his lap to hide the trembling. "I'm sorry about the dramatic manner of your arrival, but it couldn't be helped." Maybe this was a bad idea after all.

"I'm Dr. Oz Good. You can call me, Dr. Good." He set the glass on the desk. His eyes narrowed and his smooth brow creased as he frowned. "Never call me the Wizard of Oz."

Holly struggled in vain to stifle a snort. When she did let go, Dr. Good's eyes shot to her and he scowled. "Leave us, Dr. Hope." His tone was tight and disapproving.

Will looked at Holly. Her cheeks were flushed red and her eyes avoided the directors glare. She nodded her head slightly then said, "Yes, sir. I've got to check my most recent test results anyway." Holly turned left the office the doors sliding closed behind her.

Dr. Good's features relaxed and he steepled his fingers and seemed to studying him. Will was startled and jumped in the chair when Dr. Good suddenly burst out laughing. He squirmed until Dr. Good stopped and wiped the tears from his eyes with his long thin fingers. "So, Sergeant. I'm told you have a PhD in software engineering?"

Will cleared his throat. He prayed he wouldn't sound like a frog. "Uhhh, yes sir, Dr. Good...sir." I sound like the biggest idiot on the planet.

"Good. Great in fact. We need a person with your qualifications." He paused and the smile dissipated as his expression shifted to somber. "The last software engineer was...lost." He nodded and stood up behind the desk. Will detected the hesitation in his Dr. Good's voice.

Something bad must have happened, but what? "So you want me to work for you?"

Good smiled and walked around the desk and moved to sit on the sofa. He waved to Will to join him. Will sat down. "Yes, but it's up to you. Of course I will have to explain what this is all about and about our mission."

Will nodded. "Of course." This all sounds a bit cryptic. He needed answers. "Where are we?" he asked.

"I assume you've heard of Area 51?" Will nodded again and licked his lips. Aliens. These guys are nuts. "We are Area 52. Our facility, our mission, our funding, our existence is above top secret. The only people who know about us are at the top of the U.S. government. The President, the Secretary of Defense, and the Chairman of the Joint Chiefs."

His eyes narrowed and his lips formed a thin line. "No one else." He rose to his feet and began to pace the tiled floor. "Other than those who work here of course. No one knows about us, or must know about us."

Will's heart beat faster at that last part. If he told anyone about this place and the robots, he had a feeling it wouldn't be good for his health. "Ummm, Dr. Hope said something about a project?"

Dr. Good stopped pacing and turned to face him. "Our project is called TIN Men."

"By the name I'm guessing you build robots?"

Good arched one eyebrow. "That's only half the story actually."

Will arched an eyebrow. "What's the other half?"

"We're in a robot race that's been going on since 1967."

Will's curiosity threatened to bubble over. "Robot race? Like a marathon?"

Dr. Good laughed and crossed his arms over his narrow chest. "No. Not that kind of race. A cold war style race." Good dropped into silence.

Will stared back at Dr. Good uncertain what or who he was talking about. Russia wasn't the USSR, in fact the country was a shell of it's former self.

China was an economic power. Sure, they had a large military, but funding an ultra secret robot program seemed a little beyond their means. Iraq? Iran? No. No way. The Saudi's, the North Koreans? The European Union? Unlikely. "A cold war? With whom?"

"Who do you think?"

Will shrugged. "I don't know...Japan?"

Dr. Good's eyebrows rose in obvious surprise. "How did you know that?"

"I guessed."

Dr. Good moved across to this desk and picked up his glass of coke. He took a swig and offered Will a glass, which he accepted. After he filled a glass from the bottle in the bar fridge behind his desk he sat once again in the red leather executive chair.

He explained. "As you know Japan has become a technologically advanced society. Many Japanese have a love for science fiction, and robots, giant monsters. They started a giant robot program, so in order for the United States to keep it's technological edge we began ours at the same time."

Will snorted. "You do realize how stupid that sounds, right?"

"Yes, I know. But we have been in a race with the Japanese ever since. There are unconfirmed rumors that India and China have begun early work on their own robot programs, but our latest intelligence reports say they're years away from a practical working prototype."

Will stood he'd had enough. "You know this all sounds crazy. We're talking about robots!" He moved to the desk and stood staring at Dr. Good. "It's science fiction. It's not real."

Dr. Good eased back in his chair causing the leather to squeak. He arched an eyebrow. "You met, Randall, and saw the worker drones in the corridors did you not?"

Will grimaced. He was right of course. As unbelievable as it sounded the robots were real. But was everything else he said also true? "OK, Dr. Good, I'll concede that point, but I find it hard to believe a robot cold war has been going on for over forty years, and no one knows about it."

"We have developed a drug that wipes selected memories of anyone who comes into contact with our facility or research."

Will sensed Good was hiding something from him, though hiding wasn't the correct term. A better term would be evasion.

He wasn't answering his questions directly. For the first time in a long time, Will knew he was being tested. And this made him mad. He'd hated tests since Mrs. Chopnik sprang that surprise arithmetic test on his first grade class.

"Listen, Dr. Good, let's stop beating around the mechanical bush and you tell me what's going on and why I'm here."

Dr. Good surprised him when his narrow features broke into a wide smile. Had he said something funny? Or had he just sounded so stupid all a person could do was laugh at him.

"Dr. Arnett, welcome aboard." He stood behind his desk and held out his right hand.

Will took Dr. Good's hand in his. His skin was warm and the grip was firm. But what had he just joined? Will released his grip and sat down again. "Dr. Good, please tell me something important. I've come aboard what exactly?" He blurted out the last word. His frustration meter had gone through the roof.

Dr. Good's expression became very serious. "I'm offering you a chance to join Project TIN Men as the lead software development engineer. It is quite an honor, believe me.

You'll lead a team of ten of the best software engineers in the world, and you'll be paid more than Google or Microsoft or Facebook would ever pay you. I can say with no exaggeration in one year you'll make enough to buy your own private island. And you'll have enough money to buy a lifetime supply of those chocolate mint patties you love so much. Honestly? You could buy the company that makes those confections."

Will took a sip of the coke and then dragged in a deep breath. The soda tickled his taste buds and its sweetness lingered in tongue even after he swallowed. He released the breath, "What's the catch?"

Dr. Good's lips formed a tight smile. "Good. Direct. I like that." He paused and looked away. With his back now to Will he said, "We will transplant your brain into the body of a robot much like Randall so you won't require air or water. Not where you're going. Then you'll travel to the moon where you'll help to build a base on the dark side of the moon."

Will's heart raced. Moon base? His brain?

***

Two months later, Will lay on an operating table waiting for the electrodes to be affixed to the four input terminals surgically implanted in his skull.

The terminals were inserted into his frontal lobe, parietal lobe, occipital lobe, and temporal lobe. His brain wouldn't actually be removed and placed in the robots control center, but somehow the scientific team had found a way to transfer every experience, every memory, every instruction accumulated in his lifetime to the robots artificial brain.

His body would be stored in stasis while he went to the moon. The dark side of the moon to be exact. The team would be composed of seventeen robots and the base would take six months to complete.

He was pleased, Holly would be accompanying, her transferred brain also encased in a robot body.

He'd been fully briefed on the mission. They were to build a base on the dark side of the moon hidden from Earthly eyes. The reason he'd been given was the base was being built by an international organization funded by the G25. The funding was secret and the project was secret. The organization was code named The International Network or T.I.N.. The code name for the bot's was TIN Men.

He was not only chosen for his expertise in his field, but because his parents died in a car accident two years ago, he was an only child, and had no other family.

He'd begun to enjoy being a part of something. In the army he had felt more like an outsider, the regular grunts detested soldiers who were smarter than they were.

To be honest most gerbils were smarter than most of the men and women he served with in the recon unit he'd been assigned to.

While for the most part the story rang true, Will, still thought there were gaps in the tale that bothered him. Holly had admitted her reservations as well after they'd slept together. She had been working at MIT when she was approached as asked to join the project. She'd agreed when she was advised Dr. Good was the project director.

An interesting factoid about her was she was also an orphan like himself. In fact everyone he'd encounter involved with the project had no family. He couldn't shake the uncomfortable thought this meant they wouldn't be missed if something went wrong.

But what could go wrong? Their brains were transferred to living machines, then they'd slip through an energy field that transmitted matter thousands of miles in the blink of an eye.

A matter transmitter terminal was already on the moon near the site where the base would be constructed.

The European-China Space Agency had sent a robot space craft with the terminal aboard to the moon and by all reports it landed safely. Some worker droids were to set up the terminal. Recent orbital surveys confirmed the droids had completed the set up. But the real question was had the droids put it together properly.

The worker droids could have built the moon base as well, but it would have taken them decades due to their limited ability to adjust to unexpected situations. They were only capable of being programmed to respond to pre-determined situations. And not every situation could be covered by the programmers

Dr Good had been evasive about why they needed to work so fast and take such risks, but Will suspected there was much more going on than he knew.

Also, any breakdowns wouldn't be fixed, the resources hadn't been supplied to fix any mechanical problems if the droids broke down. Yet.

But this was all about to change. The plan was for the TIN men to build a repair facility as the first phase of the project.

"All TIN men to the departure bay!" said a deep male voice over the facility wide public address system.

Will set the giant robot in motion and walked the massive tunnels headed for the departure bay. Holly's lime green and soft gray two tone bot joined him. He was pleased to see her.

"Hi, Holly, you ready?"

Her bot swiveled it's head to face his and nodded. "For sure. But I wish they'd refer to us females as TIN women."

We'd been having this discussion for months but it was a spurious argument because the robots were sexless. The human sexual urges and feelings of the brain implanted in the artificial brain wasn't relevant. Especially as we communicated by telepathic means and were about to enter an inhospitable environment. In such a place sex where wasn't relevant, and these bodies weren't built with the right bits and pieces anyway.

"Next time, Ok?" Will joked.

Holly chuckled. "Yeah, okay."

We soon arrived in the departure bay where the transport technician had set up the first test of the matter transmitter. There were going to be five tests before they were sent through.

First they would send a Camera and Recording Bot, or CRB, to monitor the reception terminal.

The CRB central processor and sealed camera was built on a platform set on rubber composite tracks. Immediately upon arrival on the moon it would move off the platform then send pictures back of the remaining tests. Of course if no signals came back this would mean the droids had failed to set up the receiving transport receiver properly.

Will watched the technicians guide the robot onto the large round platform that rose above the shiny tile floor of the bay. Near the outer walls were five consol's where technicians sat monitoring everything from energy levels of the matter transporters systems, to humidity, and the telemetry data provided by a satellite net transmitted from high earth orbit to a network of satellites orbiting the moon. This would be their lifeline until the job was complete for Will and Holly and the rest of the team. There were going to be six of us building the station.

Will and Holly watched as the technicians called out data they received from their consol's as a humming sound began to grow in intensity. Finally the humming reached its zenith and there was a brilliant flash of light that seemed to consume the CRB. When the light dissipated the bot was gone.

"Sir!"

It was one of the telemetry technicians calling to Dr. Good who stood across the room at another console watching the power level indicators. He was really proud of the fact they had finally harnessed the power of a nuclear reactor that generated more power than the Hiroshima bomb. He'd been working on it since the project began in 1967.

Dr. Good looked up. "Yes? What is it, Jamal?"

"Sir. There is no signal from the CRB."

Dr. Good's brow wrinkled and Will recognized the confusion on his narrow features. "Give it a few minutes."

Suddenly the technician yelled out. His face paled and he waved one hand wildly at the screen in his consol. "Sir. You better come look at this."

Dr. Good nodded and stuffed his hands in the pockets of his ankle length white lab coat. He walked casually across the room seemingly unconcerned over the urgency in Jamal's tone. Will noted his brow was knitted and he was humming, both signs he was in reality worried. Will sensed something bad had happened.

Will moved his robot body closer to the console and at an angle he could see the screen. what he saw made him, for the first time, reconsider his reasons for agreeing to be part of this project.

On the screen he could see a wide view of a field of gray rock and sand under an ink black sky dotted with points of unblinking light. There were also blackened shards of metal scattered like leaves across the moon's surface. From the angle of the image Will suspected the camera was on its side.

It was clearly evidence of an explosion. Now Will was worried. The only thing that could explode was the nuclear power source for the transmitter reception terminal, and the internal power source for the droids. The good thing was the camera aboard the CBR had survived the explosion which meant the mostly likely source of the explosion was a droid.

The root of this problem was how this had happened. Was it coincidental the arrival of the CBR occurred at the exact moment of a droid exploding. And was the transporter terminal damaged by the explosion.

Dr. Good crossed his arms and studied the screen his features scrunched in a scowl. "I wasn't expecting this so soon."

"Dr. Good," piped up Holly's bot. She had approached the console from the opposite side from where Will was standing. "What were you expecting?"

Will thought her tone was harsh, but he too was surprised Dr. Good had withheld information from them. "Yes, doc, Holly and I want what's going on."

Dr. Good sighed and his shoulders sagged. He took off his wire rimmed glasses and massaged the bridge of his nose with his thumb and forefinger as if he had a headache, his eyes were closed. Suddenly he stopped and grunted as he put his glasses back on.

He reached for the com system button on the consol and punched the red button which changed to green meaning the public address system had been activated.

"Attention all TIN Men Project personnel, this is Dr. Good." He paused and took in a deep breath then continued. "I've been asked a rather important question and while I'm forbidden to reveal certain facts recent events on the moon lead me to believe you must all know why we must build the base on the moon and maintain absolute secrecy.

"I'm certain you have all been wondering about the rumored hidden agenda. I appreciate you have all followed orders without question while bringing this project to fruition. If we fail in our endeavors we, meaning all of humanity, will be faced with a future too terrible to imagine at the hands of a megalomaniac bent on total world domination.

Dr. Good glanced at Will's bot then his eyes drifted to Holly's. "Our TIN Men will be the front line in this war. A war against a secret organization calling itself The Mayday Directorate. The leader of The Mayday Directorate is a brilliant scientist named Dr. Bartholomew Good, my brother."

***

Will heaved the large gray and black rock across the moonscape. In the one sixth Earth gravity it flew more than a thousand yards before landing in a cloud of moon dust. They would have the area where they'd sink in the foundation posts for the new base cleared in a couple of hours. Will and the rest of the TIN Men had only been here for ten hours and already the base construction was well underway.

Holly was with a team of the surviving droids extracting ice from the shaded sides of craters. They would place the ice in the evaporation tank two of their colleagues were busily constructing. Once the tank was powered up the ice would melt and provide fresh water for the base's eventual inhabitants.

They'd waited for three months until a force of armed TIN Men could be built to provide security for the base construction.

Will wasn't happy to see an armed presence but The Mayday Directorate had been prevented from doing any further sabotage.

It was discovered that their agents had planted bombs inside some of the worker droids. Though a couple exploded when the CBR went through the matter transporter they hadn't damaged the device so severely as to stop the transport of a repair crew of droids.

After the repairs Will, Holly and the rest of the team had been sent to the moon and work had begun.

Dr. Good explained that his brother and he had started the project at Area 52 together, but his brother and he had a falling out. He hadn't heard of his brother until The Directorate destroyed the Columbia space shuttle.

Once the moon base was completed it would begin it's real work. It would be the jumping off point to send deep space missions throughout the solar system to find minerals and water and other building blocks for the eventual exploration of planets where the first signs of extraterrestrial life had been discovered.

Will was excited about the future and hoped his TIN man would survive for many years to come so he could be part of the next great adventure. Humankind was going to finally make it's mark in the galaxy.

Will stopped working when the ground began to shake. He hoped it was a meteor strike but then the early warning meteor detection grid would have alerted them of an impending strike. He had a sinking feeling he knew what caused the disturbance of the moon's crust.

Suddenly the horizon lit up with gold and red flashes. There was no denying it they were being attacked. And the TMD bots had used cloaking technology in the past but every time it had been scouts and they were quickly destroyed by the TIN Men security team. Somehow this felt different.

Will had to brace the bot's legs to keep from falling over when the ground heaved beneath him and a cloud of dust shot into the star studded sky to the west of his position. The gray dust quickly blocked out the stars. Will knew the weapon ports Dr. Good had installed in his robot were about to become useful. He had hoped to avoid the coming conflict. The directorate didn't want to talk, they wanted to destroy. Now it was war.

The TMD was planning to stop them before they could complete the moon base. Holly told him they were paid by a coalition of pirate states led by the Texas Syndicate and the Welsh Dominion. They were paying TMD to destroy the TIN Men project.

They planned to take over the interstellar exploration of deep space, not for peaceful purposes, but for conquest and monopolizing resources.

They had to be stopped, and the TIN Men had to do it.

"Sentry Seven reporting a breach in the defensive line. There are three —" The com went silent. Sentry Seven had been taken out."

It was time for action. Will sent a message through the com net. "Dr. Arnett to TIN Men and all sentries. Initiate plan alpha-two-nine."

Will counted acknowledgements and realized fourteen sentries had been lost already. Will walked to the edge of worksite and stopped. Clouds of moon dust had risen to blot out the star field across the horizon.

He'd deploy the laser gun in the left arm of the robot then the rail gun with the armor piercing projectiles in the right arm. He also engaged the energy shield that he hoped would hold off the TMD bot's weapons long enough so he could launch a counter attack. Unfortunately the weapons had been deployed so quickly the testing of the shields had been inconclusive. Will wanted to shudder at the memory of the chest plate of the test bot melting and fusing the torso.

The plan was to deploy the TIN Men and the surviving sentries in an oval shape and guard the base by repelling any attacks. The sentries were smaller therefore they'd be in front of the TIN Men who were taller and better armed. It was a classic order of battle design used by the British (though they used squares not ovals), and the Roman legions before them.

Soon Will counted thirty five sentries and looking around he saw his six companion TIN Men, including Holly who was directly behind him facing outward, her back to him. He worried she would get hit, but Dr. Good's armor should protect her. He hoped.

Then sentries quickly deployed per the plan and there was an uneasy lull. Silence no com traffic as they waited for the enemy. If Will's TIN Man could smell it would smell the sweat, the oil and grease and the heat of the laser warming to firing temperature. But since the suits didn't allow for such sensory data he would just imagine it.

Suddenly from over the horizon six large TMD robots appeared. Their armored bodies were black and silver and from the look of them they appeared to have missile launchers affixed to their left shoulders and rail guns attached to their right arms. This wasn't going to be an easy fight. The other Dr. Good had obviously anticipated the TIN Men's weapons and tactics.

This was further supported by their spreading out so as not to create one massive target. They'd be in range in ten seconds.

Time seemed to pass slower as Will silently counted down the seconds. His targeting scanner beeped and he pressed the firing button for the rail gun. The first hardened steel/titanium projectile shot off the rail and tracked to the target, one of the enemy bots to his right. The projectile struck enemy bot in the center of it's chest plate and it shot backward off it's feet. It landed in a cloud of moon dust broken in half at the waist. the legs wouldn't work without the torso.

Will was pleased. One shot, one bot out of action. This wasn't going to be such a difficult battle after all.

A flash of a laser beam shot across the no mans land from one of the enemy bots. It struck Dr. Helen Taskers TIN Man and sliced her torso in two. It was almost as if her shields weren't on.

"Will." It was Holly. "I've picked up a low frequency wave that's interfering with our shield generators." She paused and the information sunk in. If the enemy was able to do this then maybe all of their systems could be compromised.

"Helen!" Will called.

"Yes," Helen said her voice trembling with fear.

"Check your generator power level."

There was a short pause then she replied, "It's reading zero. And it's not related to the damage I've sustained."

Now Will was worried. The enemy had the upper hand, but the question was how had they learned to defeat their shields so easily? They still had the EMP weapon if the battle became hopeless. The electro magnetic pulse would take out the enemy, but would also immobilize the TIN Men. And it might wipe the neural connectors. Theoretically the EMP might result in brain death for the TIN Men as well as the enemy so it had to be a weapon of last resort. His orders from Dr. Good were simple: do not lose. He was in charge. He was determined to win this battle at all costs. The future was at stake.

A soft beep told him the enemy robots were now in range. He issued an order. "All TIN Men fire at will."

Will and the other TIN Men launched everything they had at the approaching enemy force. Their missiles and lasers struck the enemy bots and knocked them backward. The five remaining enemy robots were down. It had been easy — too easy."

"Cease fire," Will ordered.

When the first enemy robot suddenly stood up, Will's arterial heart rate increased. It looked unharmed from the missile impact.

Oh, oh, no champagne and caviar for us tonight. Celebrations for an easy victory would have to wait. They could shoot them again ,but Will suspected this would be as ineffective as the first time.

"All TIN Men, stand your ground and be ready to deploy close quarter weapons." The acknowledgements came back as Will changed his laser to a ten foot long titanium sword shaped blade. The others too had their bladed weapons at the ready.

The enemy robots had started moving again only this time they were covering more ground. They were quickly taking long sustained strides. Will knew the other TIN Men would keep fighting until the end.

Another laser sliced Allisters robot in half at the waist. Will's mood darkened. He suspected now they had a plan. They were immobilizing the TIN Men but not destroy the fused human AI brain. They would transplant the fused brain into a new robot body they could control. It was the worst possible scenario. The loss of free will.

"Allister?"

"I'll be okay, Will. A little crazy glue and I'll be right as rain."

Will smiled inside. Allister was such a joker. "No, worries, old buddy. We'll get you fixed up as soon as we have these bastards taken care of."

"Thanks, Will."

Suddenly the enemy attacked.

Will fought back clashing with the nearest enemy bot. He quickly separated an arm from the upper torso of an enemy bot with a single swipe of his blade. It was then he noticed one of the enemy bots hanging back from the others. He watched with horror as it pressed a button on a panel on it's right arm and suddenly he lost control of his body. Now he was a brain trapped in a non-functioning robot body. He was unable to move. I have to move. I can't let them win.

He stole a glance at Holly and saw she had retracted her blade and moved her robot to stand beside the enemy bot that had taken them all out of action. Will sent a command to the EMP weapon he'd secreted in one of the sentry bots. No, not Holly! Will wanted to cry.

His body jerked as if struck by lightning and the world around him disappeared.

***

When Will's systems came back on line he found himself laying on his back on the moon's surface staring up at the star strewn milky way galaxy.

He tested his robot's limbs and found everything worked.

Getting to his feet he looked around and saw the remaining TIN Men were also getting to their feet. All expect, Holly who lay still on her back next to the leader of the TMD attack force.

He knew without asking their systems were fried and their AI brains along with all their memories were wiped clean.

Dr. Good had been correct. There was a traitor in their ranks, who had not only sabotaged the worker bots in an attempt to destroy the CBR thus jeopardizing the mission. And this same traitor that provided the frequency of their shields to the enemy. Dr. Good hadn't thought they'd be able to do this unless they had help from an insider with the highest security level. Will didn't think anyone on the team could be a traitor. Especially not Holly. He'd been wrong.

Holly. Will didn't know why she did it, but one day he'd find out. When Holly's brain died her body stored in stasis back on Earth became an empty shell. She was gone forever.

Will was determined to ensure one day the other Dr. Good would pay for her death and the destruction he'd caused.

Only Dr. Good and he knew they're robot bodies had been hardened against EMP attack. The trap had worked perfectly. It had brought the traitor out into the open. Too bad it turned out to be Holly.

"Will?" It was Allister.

"Don't worry, Allister, and you too, Helen. We'll get you both fixed up. I can't have you slacking off. We have a lot of work to do still."

Helen spoke next. "Sorry, about Holly, Will."

"It's no ones fault but hers," Will said and he meant it.

The TIN Men would survive and they would compete their task. Former Technical Sergeant Will Arnett was determined to make it happen.

Strange Bedfellows

I HATE THIS PLACE.

No, I wasn't trying to swim away from the island we'd been stranded on for the past six weeks. I just wanted a few minutes alone. Besides if I tried to swim away I'd either be cut to pieces on the sharp coral off shore or be eaten by sharks. Never mind the very real possibility of drowning.

With my head bobbing in the rolling blue-green surf surrounding me, I gazed at the sand of the beach that stretched out before me like a golden line in the ocean. The palm trees and ragged under brush beyond the beach seemed to stick out of the ocean itself.

Valentine and Alice sat with their hands flat in the sand behind them watching me from the beach on the small island where we were shipwrecked six weeks ago. The flesh of their exposed faces, arms, and hands were now glowed red form the blistering tropical sun.

The roar of the wild pacific striking the razor sharp coral five hundred yards behind me made communication with my wife, or our new friend, impossible. At any moment a moray eel, great white shark, or some similar monster of the deep, would swallow me whole and they would be unable to help me. Not that I was particularly worried. We'd not been fortunate enough to see such creatures in the lagoon in the time we'd been stranded here.

I'm not a strong swimmer, so my arms and legs were beginning to ache from the exertion, and my skin was beginning to wrinkle like some orange that has been in the sun too long. Too much desk time in my old life, I mused.

With my belly hanging over my faded gray shorts, and salt water invading my mouth, ears, and eyes, I began my methodical stroke, stroke, stroke toward the shore.

Not that I wanted to go back, I just had very little choice..

Finally I was able to stand in the lapping waves. I dropped my feet to the wet sand as schools of tiny red, green, and blue fish tickled at my ankles and my feet.

My legs felt heavy beneath me as I wadded ashore. Once I was out of the water the hot sand burned the soles of my feet as I made my way, complaining with every step, toward the spot where the two women watched me, their eyes bored, their expressions listless.

Alice offered me a weak smile when I sat down beside her with a grunt. My wide butt caused a mini-shower of sticky sand that doused her hair and clothes. Lately our relationship had been more rocky than smooth sailing. As our chance of rescue diminished so it seemed did our marriage.

"Oh, com'on," she growled as she tried without success to brush the grains of sand off her ample calves.

"Sorry," I said with a shrug. What was I going to say? It's not like I invented sand.

Alice grunted not looking at me. She must have sensed my apology wasn't exactly sincere, which it wasn't.

"Nice swim?" she asked equally insincerely.

"No." I shifted my butt and felt pinching grains of sand work their way into my groin area. It was impossible to get rid of the stuff entirely. "I can't get this sand outta my nooks and crannies no matter what I do," I said.

"Stop complaining, Rob," said Val chastised me . "You're giving me a headache."

Valentine (who preferred to be called Val) had been on the sail boat with us when it went down. The skipper had disappeared in the storm.

I caught Alice's eye with a glance. She arched an eyebrow at me and shrugged her wide shoulders. Her once smooth skin was becoming rough from the weeks of being stranded on this island. It was as if we were under assault by an army of sun, wind, and salt fairies. Very soon we'd all be one big piece of red leather.

I was really beginning to hate these two as much as the island. The tension between us had grown with each passing day rescue failed to arrive.

I gave my head a shake. I was loosing it for sure.

Our new friend, Valentine Motts, was a woman of substance in the real world, as she called it. "I'm a player," she explained on day one on this speck of sand in the south pacific. She said she was also low on her meds. What kind of meds she needed and what a player was exactly she never bothered to explain and I never bothered to ask.

I suspected her lack of medication was the reason for her increasingly irritability.

"Let's go back to camp," I said, "I think we've had enough surf and sand for one afternoon don't you think?"

Val snorted her disgust then stood and began to brush the clinging sand off her cut offs and the arms of her white sleeveless blouse. Her long legs, indigo eyes, and heavy bosom attracted me to her the moment I laid eyes on her. The first time was six weeks ago when we woke up on the sand after the storm pounded the sailboat into the reef. The waves chopped the boat into kindling. In the dark we abandoned ship and swam for our lives. I still don't know how we survived the swim in the dark, but I do recall waking up to see Val, her wet clothes clinging to her voluptuous figure, lying on her side in front of me.

Out of the corner of my eye I caught Alice looking at me. Her smooth pinkish forehead was creased and her dark eyes burned a hole in me.

"What's the matter?" I said feigning ignorance.

Val had already headed for our makeshift camp above the tide line. Her footsteps muffled by the sand quickly retreated into the distance.

"You know what." Alice glared at me then stomped off her arms folded across her sagging breasts hidden beneath the green floral blouse she'd saved from the wreck.

She's more a stuff person than I am. Her feet were half buried in the soft sand as she walked away to leave me alone. My heart ached as I watched her go. How could she think this about me? Not that I hadn't given the idea of banging Val some thought these past few weeks, but it was stupid to think I'd actually do it. Alice knew I loved her. Didn't she?

I ran after my wife slipping on the sand like some drunken sailor on a weekend pass. I managed to mentally block out the searing heat of the sand as I ran.

I came up beside her. "Listen. Alice," I said breathing hard from the excretion. "It's not what you think —"

"Does it matter?"

"It does to me," I protested.

She stopped as we reached the brown earth bordering the beach. Her arms were still crossed across her smallish bosom and her eyes were filled with fire. "So?"

"What? I didn't do anything."

"You will." With that she walked off.

I watched her go knowing she was right. Or at least I wanted to, if Val wanted to. I can't imagine why she would want to sleep with a fat old fart like me, but desperate times make strange bedfellows.

***

Sitting with our backs to the ocean we watched in silence the crackling yellow and gold flames that leapt into the starlit sky. Our nightly fire consisted of palm tree logs that filled the air with dense pungent smoke.

I sat huddled between the two women on a log big enough to hold the three of us we'd dragged from the nearby forest of tall palm trees to act as our surrogate couch. We were seated upwind from the sooty, thick smoke of the fire carried in-land by the swirling winds coming off the ocean.

"One more day," said Val. Her tone was melancholy, filled with regret. I knew different. She didn't have choices any more than I did.

"Maybe we should split up?" suggested Alice. She used a stick she'd picked up from the chalky soil to poke at a burning log. This caused sparks to fly as if they were fire flies in some mad dance. The wood crackled loudly with each thrust of the stick.

"It won't do any good," said Val. Her gaze washed over me and I saw her eyes briefly flair then return to looking at a lump of burnt wood next to the fire. She wanted me. I knew it. Or was I imagining it? The hot sun and the thirst had made me doubt my sanity.

What was I going to do? My stomach began to complain and a vague taste of bile entered my mouth.

I moved to the lean-to we used to store the supply of coconuts and fruit we'd managed to collect from the trees and bushes farther in-land. I took half of one coconut and a piece of fruit that looked and tasted like a mango. I don't know if that's what it was, but it tasted okay, and it hadn't made me ill. Unlike some of the other fruit on this island I'd tried.

"Get me some water," said Alice turning to look at me.

"What do we say when we want something?" I said.

Her brow wrinkled and her eyes narrowed. "If you don't want to, just say so."

"OK. Ok…" I waved her off before I got yelled at. What's the use? I'm whipped and I know it. I set the coconut and the fruit down on the log and when to the bucket we kept in a nest of bushes to keep it out of the sun. It couldn't stay cool but it wouldn't be too warm either.

We'd managed to find a lime green plastic bucket from the boat that washed up on the beach a few days after the storm. Wreckage had washed up almost every day for the next two weeks after were stranded here.

We filled the bucket each morning with fresh water from a creek we found. The creek was close to the steep cliffs that guarded the lone mountain at the center of the island.

We had decided to keep our camp close to the beach and ferry the water from the creek because we didn't want chance missing any rescue boats or planes that might be looking for us. About as likely a possibility as my suddenly looking like Mr. Universe.

I picked up one of our three makeshift coconut drinking cups and filled it from the bucket. Once the coconut meat was removed it made a perfectly serviceable cup.

Alice didn't look up as I handed her the cup and sat down between them again. I began to work on my fruit. The sweet mango added much needed moisture to my mouth. Alice sipped at the water.

"There are caves nearby," said Val breaking the silence. "Near the cliffs. I saw them the other day when I was walking near there."

I nodded. "Yeah, Alice. Caves. We can take shelter in them."

Alice shot a look of indignation at me. "Why do you always have to agree with her?"

Val's face looked suddenly redder. She picked up a branch from the pile of kindling we'd accumulated and like Alice started to poke away at a log in the fire. The wood crackled and flames leapt skyward.

I got up. This was ridiculous. We could handle this. We should handle this. Like adults. What we'd been doing up to now was acting like teenagers with petty jealousies.

I walked to the edge of the fire's circle of light then turned to face the two warring parties. They sat as far from each other as possible without falling off the end of the log.

"Listen, ladies. I know a little something about conflict resolution through negotiation, it's a technique called —"

"Oh, not that crap again," said Alice rolling her eyes heavenward. "He's always going on about this junk. He calls it the healing circle. Well, let me tell you something, sweetheart, it doesn't work, especially in this situation." She pointed an accusatory finger at Val.

Alice stopped speaking, her jaw was set in a determined line and her eyes were moist but scowled at me.

Val's eyes too burned with anger. She tossed the stick to the ground and whirled on the log to face Alice.

"I've listened to just about all I want to from you, Alice. I thought we'd all become friends, then a few days ago you seemed to think your husband and I...well, it doesn't matter what you thought. You're just wrong that's all. I'm not who you seem to think I am, and frankly I resent your insinuations."

With that Val stood and disappeared into the darkness headed in the direction of the beach. The night black as ink since there was no moon tonight. I could feel the breeze pick up an increase in wind speed suddenly brushed my cheeks. The wind pressed greasy hair flat against my forehead

The air smelled of ozone so I knew a storm was coming. A big storm like the one that stranded us here.

So not good.

***

Sure enough the wind had turned into a howling gale by dawn. Rain the size of small cats pelted us as Alice and I huddled side-by-side under the wooden lean-to our hands wrapped around our knees. When we were younger we would have been hugging each other but the tension had evaporated those urges. But Alice refused to go to the caves and I was determined to support her.

Regardless none of this helped.

The palm fronds we'd used to construct the roof were quickly swept away by the high winds. The surf pounded the beach with a deafening roar. Bits of sand filled our mouths our eyes and our throats. It seemed like the end of the world.

"Where's your girlfriend?" said Alice in my left ear, her lips within inches of me. The rain drops stung my exposed areas of flesh and my eyes were blurred by sheets of rain that came from the thick, black clouds overhead. The air was occasionally split by peels of thunder and bolts of brilliant white and gold lightning lighted up the midnight clouds making them glow.

"She's not my girlfriend," I said, exasperated by her unrelenting attitude.

Alice sighed heavily and her shoulders drooped. "Yeah. I suspected as much."

Didn't she understand I loved her? I made one tiny mistake and it was over?

My eyes swept the deserted beach. It was covered with white foam due to the towering black waves of immense size and ferocity of the waves that rolled in over the reefs. The once calm lagoon had become a steaming chaos. "And before you ask. I don't know where she went."

Alice looked into my eyes and I saw the hard edge evaporate in her eyes.

We grabbed each and hugged tightly as if we never wanted to be apart ever again. We hadn't been this close in a long time and it felt good. If we died now I do so as a happy man. We broke our hug and she pressed her lips to mine. I kissed her back my heart pounding hard in my chest. We were like newly weds again.

***

By afternoon the rain had been reduced to slanted sprinkles of warm tap water and the wind had blown itself into a gentle breeze. We shivered in our wet clothes as we huddled under our re-built lean-to.

I decided I better find out what happened to Val. I hoped she hadn't been swept out to sea. If that were the case no one would ever find her body.

I stood and brushed the clingy sand off my body as best I could, then ran my hand over the scraggy, gray beard I had grown these past weeks.

"You stay here, Alice," I said, my voice low surprising even me with its intensity.

Alice gave a dubious look, but I knew she was tired and wanted to enjoy a nap now the weather had improved somewhat. She nodded and her mouth formed a gentle smile. She then laid her dirty blonde hair on her folded arms and closed her eyes. I knew she'd be in dreamland in no time.

As I left the lean-to I looked up at the forest covered mountain side disappearing into the boiling clouds. The mountain peak was normally visible on clear days was obscured by the ink black clouds surrounding the peak. I'd taken to thinking of this silent monolith as ours. I shook my head.

What the hell was I thinking? We're not Tarzan and Jane.

Val had said there were caves at the base of the cliffs, and that those caves might be a better place to hole up than here on the beach. Given what Alice and I had just experienced I was thinking she might be right. Maybe Val had taken her own advice and was right now holed up in one of them waiting out the storm.

I didn't recall seeing any caves in our treks inland but they could certainly be there.

We'd salvaged some rope from the shipwreck, which I used to strap palm leaves to my feet to protect them from the sharp volcanic rocks strewn throughout the forest. It was a technique we'd learned on our early days on forays for food and water. The broad leaf palm leaves were tough and made excellent insulation.

I then started into the woods and was soon out of sight of the beach. As I trudged through the thick undergrowth birds called to each other in the trees overhead.

I sniffed the air and thought I detect the scent of smoke in the air. It was very faint, and came from my left. It was likely due to a lighting strike that had ignited some of the forest. The hard rains of earlier today would have quickly doused the flames, however, this afternoon I wasn't so sure.

Good thing the smell was so faint or I'd be more concerned. I would hate to be stuck on the beach if the weather all of a sudden turned worse again. Tropical storms were tricky things to predict.

After several exhausting minutes I stopped to sit on a fallen tree. My back hurt, my feet hurt, and my neck hurt.

"There you are," said a whispered voice from behind me. I whirled around on the log. Nothing. Maybe I was hearing things —

"Hello, Rob," whispered the sultry voice.

I turned my head quickly immediately regretting the sudden jarring of my already sore neck. My pain was rewarded by the sight of Val in all her barely clothed glory. Her eyes glowed with an inner light that made me sweat. My mouth dried and licked my lips.

"Val, I've been looking for you —"

"And I for you," she breathed making my heart beat harder against my rib cage.

She came toward me slowly at first then faster. She moved quicker than anyone I've ever seen until she stood over me her glowing eyes gazing down at me where I was seated on the tree trunk rubbing my sore feet.

"Listen, Val, there's some junk we need to clear up between us and Alice. I mean com'on there's no us now is there? One time doesn't count."

Val paused and her eyes fixed on mine. My stomach jumped with fear. There was something different about her eyes. I felt a chill run through my soul.

"You seriously think that was sex." She laughed harshly at my puzzled expression. "What nonsense. I bit you. I didn't mean to, but it's too late now. Its not something you can exactly take back you know."

"What….?" I felt the blood drain from my face. Bit me? What is she talking about? "I may be a 'wham bam thank you ma'am kind of guy, but I'm definitely not into the kinky stuff. I thought we had sex. In fact I'm pretty sure…." I paused. Hold on. Was my memory playing tricks on me? "...maybe not."

Val smiled and as she did I noticed her canine teeth were longer than the rest of her perfect white teeth. Val has model teeth. The kind Madison Avenue likes for TV toothpaste commercials.

I stared at her teeth and she snapped her mouth shut.

"I'm sorry, Rob. I should have told you two the truth about me."

I nodded. "I know you have a medical condition that requires measured doses of a drug I've never heard of. But since I'm not a medical doctor what do I know about it. The drug controls powerful urg…" My words trailed off as the revelation struck me as if I'd just been struck by lightning. "You're a vampire? Com'on. It's absurd. There are no such things. Vampires are a myth."

"Actually it's not a myth. There are people with rare blood disorders that cause them to have the urge to drink blood. My line has a genetic abnormally we control with drugs. My family became wealthy when we cornered the market on the drug and began to produce it in sufficient quantities."

I shook my head. "I still don't get it. What happens if you don't take the drug?"

"Then we become what fiction and the movies would call a vampire." She moved away her head bowed. "Many of my ancestors were hunted down and murdered because of this affliction. The drug makes it possible for us to live normal, productive lives."

"But you're able to walk around in the day. How is that possible?"

She laughed and my heart skipped a beat as I caught her heady scent. My hormones were on fire from the sound of her husky voice. "If you're referring to that nonsense about sunlight killing us, crosses and holy water, and sleeping in coffins filled with dirt, that's all utter nonsense. Hollywood fantasy. We're not the un-dead." She made those little quotation marks in the air with her long fingers.

"Oh," I said. What more can I say. This was far removed from my experience. "So what do we do now? I mean your drug is obviously gone."

"We feed our addiction of course."

Have you ever had one of those moments in life where things got creepy very fast? The skin on my arms was suddenly covered in goose bumps. This was one of those moments.

"What do you mean we?"

She shook her head. "I bit you. Isn't it obvious?"

"I'm infected…." The shock of that realization hit me like a freight train, which in the end would've been kinder.

"I spiked the water with the drug which is why I ran short. Now let's get Alice. We can share." Val turned to walk off and that's when I did it. I picked up a tree branch that had been blown down in the storm and rushed at her from behind.

I'm certain she didn't know what hit her as the tapered end of the length of branch impaled her. She dropped and fell on her face to the rich soil of the forest floor with a thump and lay still. Blood drained from around the entry point for several moments until it stopped to form a pool around Val's body.

I looked down at my blood soaked hands and couldn't believe what I'd just done. I didn't think I was capable of committing murder, but as I gazed down at Val's corpse I realized that somehow my physical strength had been multiplied.

One thing about vampires was true, a stake through the heart killed them. Then again regular humans can also be killed by being impaled with a stake. I killed someone. I killed Val.

I felt a rush of adrenalin as I made my way back to camp. The storm had abated completely by now and the heated tropical sun had managed to cut through the cloud cover causing mists of white steam to form all around me as I hurried my heart pounding in my chest.

I stepped out onto the beach to find Alice wasn't alone. A group of men surrounded her. They were dressed in navy uniforms. The bow of a gleaming white launch was partially dug into the sand.

Rescue. My heart began to race. We'd been rescued!

I stopped and froze where I stood. I thought of Val laying dead back in the woods and of the vampirism she'd infected me with. There were no drugs. I'd kill again. Next time it might be Alice. Next time the person might be an innocent.

I'm no murderer. I must confess. If they lock me up then everyone will be safe.

***

I sit here on death row in my ten by six foot cell at the Texas State penitentiary awaiting my execution. Val's family has provided me with the drugs I need until my life will be ended. It's not so bad. It'll all be over soon.

Death isn't such a strange bedfellow. It's certainly preferable to life as a vampire.

Strange as it may seem Alice and I are closer now than ever in our twenty five years of marriage. I told her I killed Val to stop her from harming her. I told her I did it for love. She said she understood.

At least someone understands.

The Incredible Mr. Fix-It

HANK MUELLER STARED AT Mrs. Jones toaster through his dirt specked, wire-rimmed reading glasses perched at the tip of his hawk-like nose. His white bushy eyebrows were arched on his forehead above pale gray eyes. The toaster rested on the counter of his fix-it workshop bench in the reception area at the front of the shop facing the window overlooking the quiet street. A gray haired matronly woman stood on the other side of the counter watching him study her toaster in rapt attention, her watery eyes wide with expectation.

He eyed the switching mechanism closely as if he were a scientist gazing at a cold germ under a microscope. "Yes, he muttered to himself, "that must be…"

His heavily lined face cracked like a desert in the middle of summer when he broke into a wide grin. Mrs. Jones, the retired schoolteacher, one of his longest customers, smiled at him. Her eyes glowed with pleasure about his assessment. Her ruddy moon-shaped face beamed with joy. Her grass green eyes focused on his looking back at her.

"I'll have this ready ta go in ten minutes. I have the parts in the back," Hank assured her.

The rear storage area of the modest fix-it shop occupied most of the one story brick building near the county's only auto wrecker yard. Inside the dank storage area were stacks of sand colored moldy cardboard boxes, carefully stored and catalogued, sitting on steel shelves. Each one was filled to bursting with machine parts of all sizes and shapes scavenged by Hank over the past fifty years.

Hank had little formal education, but he'd been a tinker all his life. He could fix anything. When he was three years old, he'd removed every cupboard door in his mother's kitchen with a Phillips screwdriver. His mother was horrified, but his father, who adored his only child, laughed and had taken it upon himself to encourage his son's natural ability to tinker.

His father was a gas fitter whose greatest joy in life was the weekly swap meets.

Young Hank had often accompanied his father into the forays into the world of pink flamingos, toys, games, musty books, carved home made wood signs, carefully lacquered and engraved with a family name like Smith, or Johnson, and every do-dad and odds and sods known to man.

Hank cherished the memory of these father and son outings. The treasures he and his father rescued from obscurity quickly became a shared obsession. Monstrously large steel framed calculators, with large plastic coated steel handles and ivory colored bulky plastic buttons that made a ratcheting sound when you pulled the handle. Engines for lawn mowers, model airplane parts, and unidentifiable electrical parts, from machines too foreign for them to identify. All these came home with them on many of these trips.

Hank would spend hours in the basement of his parent's home in the workshop deconstructing these strange objects. After these weird and wonderful machines were lovingly taken apart, Hank analyzed them and studied them to find out how they worked. He also learned by experimentation to fix them if they were broken. At first, he was able to make some work as they were supposed to, while others stumped him completely.

This frustration made him work ever harder. He ached to know how things worked.

As the years went by, Hank collected more and more machines. His amassed collection soon comprised all types and sizes of devices, for every conceivable purpose known or unknown. Some didn't work when they first came home, not that this bothered Hank. He made them work. He fixed them.

As he passed through adolescence to manhood he discovered he was able to not only fix mechanical and electrical machines of all types, but in some cases he could make them better than their builders originally designed them. This became his true gift.

Hank left high school at the end of grade eleven bored by the structure and the lack of challenge inherent in formal education. He was determined to go his own way.

All through high school, Hank accepted odd jobs to fix people's machines. Teachers, housewives, his buddies, all types of people brought their bicycles, home appliances, lawn mowers, and in some cases, their cars, for Hank to fix. A few of the garages in town offered him jobs. He turned them all down preferring to accept small payments for helping his friends and neighbors.

After high school with the money he saved from these odd jobs, he bought the little abandoned auto parts shop near the wreckers yard and set up his tinker shop. He hung out a sign and became known around the county as the Incredible Mr. Fix-It, the guy who could fix anything.

Today, fifty years later, he was repairing Mrs. Jones toaster.

He shuffled into the back and studied the rows of boxes sitting on the blue steel shelves. On the top shelf, the fourth one from the bottom, he spotted the words, in his scrawled handwriting that read toaster parts. The musty smell of fifty years of accumulated dust that permeated the room didn't bother him.

He went to the corner of the room where he kept a stainless steel framed kitchen chair with a torn red vinyl seat. he hefted it and carried it the shelf where he'd found the parts he needed. Hank stood on the chair and gazed into the box. After rummaging through the oily parts, he found the switch for the same make, but the model one above Mrs. Jones' toaster, and stepped down. His worn, brown leatherwork boots squeaked in the silence of the room. He wiped his oily hands on the front of his stained, dark green coveralls.

He moved over to the wooden workbench against the opposite wall and turned on the spot light he kept attached to the bench. It was attached to a swivel assembly so pulled it toward him as he focused the yellow spot of light on the faulty switch. He pulled the proper size and type of screwdriver from the neat row of screwdrivers attached to a corkboard affixed to the wall in front of him over the bench. He removed the switch from the toaster with one deft turn of the screws then, after studying the replacement switch, and the now empty space where the old switch had been, saw that they were incompatible in size and shape.

No problem, he thought.

After ten minutes, exactly as promised, he reappeared behind the service counter to a startled Mrs. Jones who sat patiently in a chair in her navy blue, ankle length dress staring out the front window at the light rain falling across the cracked two lane paved road outside. Potholes peppered the old access road it had definitely seen better days. Hank liked to say it was as old as he looked.

"Here, Mrs. Jones," Hank said with a wide smile on his grizzled stubble covered features. His wispy white hair flew about his balding tanned head like shredded cotton in a mix master.

Mrs. Jones studied the toaster and saw the shiny new switch assembly. Somehow, it didn't look the same.

Seeing her puzzled expression Hank said, "I made it better. It'll never break again. The heating element'll last another year, but it's not worth fixing. You'll be gettin' a newin' then."

She nodded as she placed her glossy black vinyl purse on the finger print covered glass of the counter top. She pushed the gold colored latch and the purse clicked open.

"How much –" she started to say.

"Ten," he said.

She smiled warmly. She reached into the spot where she kept her household money in a side pocket, retrieved the proper bill, and placed it flat on the counter. "Mr. Jones will be so pleased. He loves his toast in the morning."

Hank nodded and picked up the ten, folded it in half then stuffed it in the left pocket of his coveralls. His customers were always saying much the same thing when he fixed their appliances, but after fifty years in the tinker business, he was becoming bored. Maybe it was time to retire.

He waved to Mrs. Jones as she bustled out the front door causing the little bell that hung off a hook over the door to chime brightly. But, he knew his ability to make people happy was the real reward for him; it was the one thing that made his life worth living.

He sighed and walked slowly into the back. He sat in the chair in front of the workbench and stared at the neat rows of screwdrivers, wrenches and other tools of his trade.

The bell over the front door interrupted his thoughts. Someone had entered the shop.

Accompanied by a creak from his knees he managed to lift himself from the chair and shuffled to the front. Two men greeted him as he entered the area behind the counter.

They were young men, the older of the two probably no more than thirty-five, the other considerably younger. The older of the two had his uniformed peaked cap tucked under his left arm. He wore a blue uniform, which meant he was in the Air Force. Hank didn't know much about the military ranks but he could tell by the expression of the other man, a blond crew cut made him look far younger than his real age, as he eyed the other man, the one smiling warmly and holding out his hand in greeting, was the more senior of the two.

His dark eyes and his dark brown crew cut made him appear like the serious military man he no doubt was.

These guys were so damned serious about every little thing, mused Hank. With their fancy razor pressed blue uniforms, spit polished brass buttons, colorful ribbons over the left breast pocket of their uniform jackets, and the gold wings over the right. They made quite a show of their superiority over lowly civilians like himself.

Hank took the offered hand and smiled thinly. "Yes. How can I help you?" he said. Letting go of the air force man's hand, he buried both hands in the pockets of his coveralls. The man dark eyes flinched a little, but the smile stayed fixed to his tanned face, as he rubbed his now oily hand down his right pant leg.

"Mr. Mueller? I'm —"

"It's Hank and I gave at the office," said Hank.

The younger man looked around seemingly unsure what Hank meant. The older of the two chuckled uneasily.

"We're not here to collect for the old pilots retirement fund if that's what you think —"

"Actually, I thought it was tickets for the air force ball. You guys 'ave one don' ya, like firemen?"

The younger man frowned as it suddenly dawned on him that Hank was pulling their collective legs.

The older man's features shifted to a tolerant smile. His eyes said he wasn't amused with Hank's attitude. "Mr. Mueller, I think we're getting off on the wrong foot. My name's Major John Kenyon," Kenyon said as he indicated the younger man standing next to him. "This is Sergeant Williams. We're here to ask you for a favor."

Hanks senses were tweaked by the Major's revelation. The air force needed my help? An old tinker from a backwater county? He thought maybe he'd better give a listen might be interesting.

"You guys want some coffee?" Before they could respond, Hank was in the back room getting his raincoat. It was dirty yellow having been in his shops work room for over thirty years. It was lined for warmth, but the heavy yellow plastic coated exterior was stained with oil and grease. He slipped his left arm in the sleeve as he walked to the front door.

"You comin'?" he said as he held the door open for the two air force men. The bell tingled in the silence of the room. Outside the rain had begun to fall harder.

The sound of the heavy raindrops hitting the gravel parking area along the road came clearly through the open door. The air was filled with the scent of wood smoke from the auto wreckers next door. Billy was again burning wood, reclaimed from the ancient cedars that ran along both sides of the road, to keep him warm in the guard shack.

The two men looked at each other uncertain if they should follow then the major shrugged and motioned for his subordinate to go ahead of him.

The sergeant placed his peaked cap on his wide square head and went into the rain. The major followed close behind. Hank smiled turned the button lock to secure the door behind them. He paused to turn the white plastic sign that hung off a hook secured to the door with a clear rubberized suction cup, in order that anyone seeing it would know he was closed.

Hank shook his head and smiled as he went outside and led them to the coffee shop not a block away. It was old one story stucco building, constructed in the same era as his tinker shop, with a half lit sign out front, the owner hadn't replaced the burned out fluorescent tubes inside the sign for the past three years. The place was called, as many similar greasy spoons across the country were, Mom's Diner.

By the time they were in the front door, and wiped their wet shoes on the dirty mat just inside the glass wood framed door, the military men's uniforms were a considerably darker blue, having been thoroughly soaked through by the rain.

The sergeant looked uncomfortably at the major who shrugged as they removed their caps and shook off the rainwater as best they could.

Hank led them to a booth by one of the large picture windows that overlooked the road. The interior was warm and dry and filled with the smelled of fresh brewed coffee and homemade vegetable soup.

The waitress, a red haired woman of about forty, her white nametag identified her as Hazel, approached them. In her red finger nailed right hand she held a green and white order pad and her light pink waitress uniform was pressed and crisp. A bleached white apron tied at the back like a Christmas package covered the front of the knee length pink skirt.

She smiled as she approached, her heavy makeup seeming to crack as she exaggerated her hip swinging, as she spotted the two uniformed men. Her painted red lips, that surrounded pure white teeth, were turned upward at the corners.

"Hey, Hank how's it hanging?" she said her voice as cheerful as her smile.

"Good, Haze. Three coffees, okay?" he said pointing at the two men who sat shivering in their damp blue uniforms.

"Thanks, Mr. Mueller," said Kenyon. The sergeant nodded eagerly in agreement. Hank smiled thinly his gray eyes sparkling with amusement.

"I gather you boys need me," said Hank as Hazel dropped three full coffee cups in front of them along with plastic covered menus, one for each of them.

Kenyon took a sip of the warm, black coffee. His complexion became flushed again as the heat inside the diner penetrated his wet exterior. He shrugged. "Yes, sir...huh, sorry, Hank. Yes, we need your special talents."

"How do you know I have special talents?" said Hank his forehead wrinkled.

Sergeant Williams unbuttoned one of his breast pockets and pulled out a brown leather bound notebook, which he flipped, open.

"Hank Mueller, born August 22, 1936 to parents Kurt and Gertrude Mueller. The Mueller's emigrated to the U.S. in 1935 to escape the rise to power of Adolph Hitler. Kurt Mueller was a gas fitter until he died in a mysterious explosion in 1967. Mother, Gertrude Miller, died five years later of natural causes." Williams paused to flip the page.

"Hank Mueller left school at the end of grade eleven to start his own tinker shop, which he has owned and operated ever since." Williams finished, and with a flourish that would've rivalled the great swordsmen of Europe, he closed the notebook.

Hank eyed them closely as if he were studying them. Finally, he said, "You guys are pretty thorough. So what about me interests you?"

"We also hear you can repair anything and I mean anything. Some say you're a magician with machines," said Kenyon. He shrugged. "Of course, you're not a magician, but you're handy with machines and that is a talent that we need. Er, which your government needs."

Hank snorted and raised his cup to his lips his twinkling eyes peering at the two military men over the cups rim. "Why should I help you? Besides, don't you guys have your own mechanics and engineers to fix things? Where are your big brains when you need 'em?"

"Huh, it's kind of complicated," said Kenyon. His cheeks flushed crimson, but this time not due to the warmth of the room.

"What you got a broken toaster, or maybe a microwave that's makin' the boys in the mess glow after dark?"

Hank saw the sergeants eyes flit at the major who cringed as Hank rattled the man's cage. But Hank just couldn't help himself. He hated government with all their paperwork and miles of red tape. All his life he'd done everything he could to avoid contact with them. Now here they were on his doorstep asking for his help. How ironic was that?

Hank didn't have kids, or a wife, so he pretty much kept to himself. He had a pretty good life going. True the challenges had been rare these past few years, but why spoil all that by getting involved with these government geeks?

Hank leaned forward his expression serious. "Listen, unless you guys tell me what you want right now I'm gonna pack my kit and head back to my shop."

"Mr. Mueller, there's no need to…" said Kenyon.

"Now, or I walk," Hank said simply giving the two men a stern glare then shrugged and began to slide out of the booth. The cushion beneath him squeaked as he slid across its smooth surface.

Kenyon raised his hand to stop him and the sergeant stared wild-eyed at the senior officer. Hank's curiosity got the better of him and he stopped at the edge of the seat cushion.

"Okay, Mr. Mueller.." Hank gave the man a withering look. "Sorry. Hank," said Kenyon, though he looked uncomfortable being so familiar with a civilian. "We have a job for you at the base. A contract really. Short term. You don't have to enlist or anything if that's what you're thinking…"

Hank snorted.

Kenyon continued. "It's a thing…we're stumped…oh hell." Kenyon appeared lost for words.

The young sergeant, after glancing around to make sure no one was listening, spoke his voice low. "Mr. Mueller, it's an object from outer space. Unlike anything we've ever encountered and we need your help. We've tried everything to make it work. I'm the best tinker in the air force and even I can't make it operate."

"Did you try kicking it?" said Hank sarcastically.

The sergeant looked perplexed by Hank's suggestion. "Huh, no actually. Do you think that'll work?" Hank had to give the boy credit he had a heap o' enthusiasm.

Hank chuckled as he slid back to sit across from the two men. "Naw, boy. I was funin' with ya. How's about we go over to the base and you show me this thing whatever it is."

They nodded with Kenyon looking none too pleased.

Hank smiled as he lifted his cup and drained the remainder o the lukewarm coffee. The sergeant looked pleased with himself until the major cast him a disparaging look.

***

An hour later, they pulled up in the regulation plain dark blue air force sedan in front of a dark abandoned hangar. Hank thought it was a Ford though it had no markings, except official ones, anywhere on the car.

The air base looked deserted for the most part, tumble weeds rolled by them and the wind carried the musty smelling desert into their nostrils through the open windows of the car. They stopped in front of the crescent shaped structure that towered upwards of five stories over their heads. Sure a biggin, thought Hank eyeing the large, dark structure.

As they stopped two figures dressed in dark green fatigues that made them near invisible each carrying an automatic rifle pointed directly at them, bracketed the car. Hank didn't know where they'd come from.

He'd not seen them as they pulled up until this very moment.

One stood in front of the car his rifle pointed at them while the other edged toward the drivers side of the car. The man in front's dark eyes scanned them, as did the barrel of his rifle, as if his hard eyes were sighting them like prey for the kill. A shiver of nervousness travel through Hank and then it was gone. He was with the two air force men. He didn't have anything to worry about. He hoped.

The second man shouldered his rifle, with a strap that was attached to the stock, and moved to the open drivers window.

Silently Kenyon handed the man a small black wallet. The man studied Kenyon's identification then held it up to check the picture against the real Kenyon. Satisfied he handed it back to the Kenyon.

"Major, I need Identification for the other two, sir."

The sergeant handed an identical black wallet to Kenyon who handed it to the grim faced guard. Hank, realizing he didn't have a little black wallet, pulled out his worn brown leather wallet from his coveralls back pocket and looked through it.

He smiled and nodded when he found what he was looking for and handed it to Kenyon who, without looking at it, handed the white plastic coated card to the guard. The guard leaned over and checked the sergeant against the picture in his wallet then gazed at Hank's id.

He handed it back to the major. "Not funny, sir." Kenyon looked at the card with a smiling picture of Hank. It was his library card that expired in 1972. Hank's hair was dark back then and covered his whole head.

"I'll vouch for him, airman."

The stone-faced airman stood back at attention then saluted. "Yes, sir." The airman nodded to his companion who lowered his rifle and with a blur of speed, they were gone. Hank couldn't see where they went. These guys were like ghosts, Houdini's, or something.

They stepped out of the car to stand in front of a black steel door. Hank didn't recall ever seeing pictures of hangars with doors like this one. It was massive and reminded him of his boyhood depictions of what the door at Fort Knox must look like.

They walked up to the door and Hank saw a stream of red light appear in front of them, which they would have to walk through to go any further.

Major Kenyon and Sergeant Williams walked through the light and with a groan of stressed metal against metal; the door began to slowly open outward. Hank hesitated watching the door begin to open. It was so damn big, he thought.

Kenyon stopped and looked back a small smile on his lips. "It's okay, Hank. The beam is a harmless low intensity-scanning device. It's perfectly safe."

Hank nodded then walked through the beam of light into the doorway created by the now open door.

Inside was a large bright room with a polished cement floor that gleamed. Hank stopped to glanced upward and saw the bare black walls that seemed to stretch forever over their heads until high above he saw the latticework of steel girders that made up the ceiling. Ahead of them was a raised platform with a tan colored service desk behind which sat two uniformed women watching them intently, their expressions hard. They wore camouflage fatigues similar to the men they'd encountered outside.

When they saw the new arrivals they stood and their hard blue eyes followed them as they crossed the open space between them. Hank could see they each had one hand resting on the butt of their pistols that hung off web belts obviously ready in case of trouble. These people are a little too paranoid, thought Hank.

The two women wore their hair up in ponytails. In black print over the right breast of their razor pressed camouflage shirts were their surnames. Norris and Lopez.

"Major," said Norris with a grim nod. Her icy expression focused on Hank. She didn't appear to appreciate civilian visitors.

"He's the IMFI," said Kenyon. Norris nodded at him her eyes expressionless. She stepped back and dropped her eyes to her seated companion. They exchanged a silent communication. What the hell was an IMFI? Hank thought for a moment then realized they meant him. Great, he thought, I've been reduced to an acronym.

At no time did she move to salute the major even though, as indicated by the two stripes on the collar of her uniform shirt, even Hank knew she was of a lower rank than either Kenyon or the sergeant. I thought they all had to salute superiors in the military.

"We're the repair team," said Kenyon.

Norris looked sceptical but she glanced at Lopez and nodded. The woman named Lopez reached beneath the counter, out of their line of sight, and flicked a hidden switch. A door appeared behind them and it slowly opened accompanied by the sound of compressed air escaping.

The two women then stood at attention eyes forward and saluted as Major Kenyon, Sergeant Williams, and a mildly amused Hank Mueller crossed the space to the open door. Kenyon and Williams returned the salutes as they headed away.

Hank suddenly realized that their footsteps should be echoing off these high walls yet there was only a slight rustling of their clothes as they moved. Something was absorbing the sound.

They entered through the door to find a lower more normal ceiling with a corridor containing a series of plain white doors than ran the length of the hallway. They seemed to stretch out for miles before them. The doors had no handles and the white tiles on the floor reflected their images as they walked. Mr. Clean must be their janitor, thought Hank. Again, there was no sound of their passage.

Kenyon stopped part way down the hallway. He reached into the right breast pocket of his uniform jacket to pull out a small sky blue card then slipped it into a barely discernible slit next to the door.

He smiled knowingly at Hank as the door slid aside into a recess in the doors frame. Hank nodded his pale gray eyes focused on the dark room they were about to enter.

"There's no turning back after we go in there," Kenyon said with a sideways glance at Williams who looked anxious.

Hank nodded silently. With all, this security whatever was in that room had to be something good and his natural curiosity, that had driven him most of his life, kicked in. He had to see it no matter what the consequences.

"Okay," said Kenyon. He reached inside the door and hit a button.

Large spotlights pierced the darkness focused on the center of the dark room where it lighted up a polished cement floor, like the one they'd seen in the other room. There, resting on a tri pod landing assembly was a ship or aircraft. Its appearance reminded Hank of a child's toy from a bygone era.

With a deliberate pace, Hank walked around the ship, which was itself round. It stood some ten to fifteen feet off the floor of the empty hangar. There were three, steel wheeled, red tool trays, each containing numerous drawers, standing off to one side as he passed on his way round the circumference of the vessel. It was obviously a space ship of some kind. An alien space ship. A big one.

A slow smile came over his face as he walked.

This was why they needed him, the Incredible Mr. Fix-It, the IMFI. He stopped in front of Kenyon and Williams with a wide grin fixed on his pale features.

"How much do you want to fix this?" said Kenyon.

Hank looked at them then at the ship. His eyes narrowed as he studied it and he rubbed his chin with his long narrow fingers in thought, finally, he said, "Nothing. I just want my chance at this baby."

Major Kenyon looked surprised while Williams beamed at him. Hank was beginning to take a shine to the little guy.

"Great," Williams said, "the NASA boys went to over this thing and over it again. They couldn't figure any of it out not even the basics. I was able to map the basic layout and…"

"That's okay, boy I'll make a tinker outta ya yet," Hank said as he placed one gnarled hand on the young man's shoulder to silence him. Hank couldn't help himself as he felt the enthusiasm emanating from this young man. It reminded him of him fifty years ago when he'd set up his shop. When the world was much younger.

"Why don't we get started," said Hank as he eyed Williams who stole a glance at Kenyon who shrugged his approval.

Kenyon then headed back out the door they'd entered through leaving the two men alone.

A ramp extended from the one section of the craft to the floor of the hangar. This would give them access to the interior. Williams walked toward the three tool stands.

" What do you need?" he said brightly.

Hank looked thoughtful then said, "I think a Phillips should do."

"Screw driver?" Hank nodded. "Anything else? We got everything.."

"Nope, just a Phillips. That's all."

Williams shrugged. "Okay, you're the boss." He reached into a drawer he'd opened and pulled out a long yellow handled screwdriver, of the size Hank suggested, which he handed to the older man. Hank took it and stuffed it in the back pocket of his coveralls.

"Say, boy what's your first name? I don't wanta be callin' ya Williams, or God help me sergeant, or some shit."

Williams smiled as he said, "Gabby, sir…"

"Hank. Please."

"Yes…Hank."

Hank slapped Gabby on the back and they laughed. They then walked up the ramp into the alien ship. It was time to get to work.

Gabby led Hank to the interior of the ship via doors that seemed to melt away as if they didn't exist as they moved through them. It was as if the ship were alive. The doors reappeared as they stood still in each room. The spacecraft contained four separate compartments with a central hub that joined them.

Gabby showed him the access hatch in the floor of one of he rooms where he'd discovered, when it was pulled back, what he speculated was the engine compartment. It wasn't very much larger than eighteen inches square. Hank studied the contents of the drive systems closely. He removed his wire-rimed glasses and wiped them on one pant leg of his coveralls. It was the only spot on the soiled garment that wasn't covered in grease or oil. He then perched them back on the end of his long nose.

"Yes, he muttered, "that must be....."

Hank stood and turned to Gabby who scrambled to stand beside him. "Okay, you have to leave now."

"But..." stuttered Gabby, "I..."

Hank placed one hand on the young man's shoulder. "It'll be okay, Gabby. You just leave me and 'ol Betsy here alone for a spell and I'll have her up and runnin' for ya. OK?"

Gabby looked like he was going to hurt himself his face so twisted with his conflicting loyalties.

"I'll teach ya ta be a real honest to God tinker if ya let me," Hank said with a sly wink.

Gabby's features told Hank he'd won. The young sergeant resigned himself to letting Hank stay here by himself. What he couldn't hide was his disappointment at not being allowed to see how Hank worked his magic.

"One step at a time, boy," said Hank.

With his shoulders, slumped Gabby left the room through the door, which solidified once he was outside. Hank smiled to himself and pulled the screwdriver out of his back pocket. He hefted the weight of the long steel shaft with the heavy plastic handle in his hand then bent down to peer into the access bay.

***

An hour later, he strolled down the ramp the screwdriver protruding from his back pocket. He had an oily handkerchief in his hands and was wiping them clean with it. He was also whistling softly to himself. The walls absorbed the sound of his out of tune whistle.

The door to the hangar burst open and Major Kenyon came rushing through followed by Gabby Williams. He stopped at the bottom of the ramp and watched Hank saunter down to meet them.

Hank's gray eyes were focused on his hands as he wiped them. He stopped in font of the two air force men.

"Well?" said Kenyon.

In response to his question, the ship began to hum softly and the metallic surface began to glow with an inner light.

"You've done it!" said Gabby, his voice that of a schoolboy on the last day of school before summer vacation.

Kenyon's eyes were wide as he stared dumbfounded at the alien ship suddenly come to life. His jaw hung open. "It can't be…" was all he managed to say.

"I'll see you boys later," said Hank with a small grin playing over his lined features. "I believe ma ride is sittin' outside?"

Gabby nodded and followed behind him like a puppy dog that smelled a treat coming.

When they were outside, and Hank seated in the back of air force car for the ride home, Gabby leaned toward car's passenger window. "You really are the Incredible Mr. Fix-It aren't you, Hank?"

"Yup," Hank said as he rolled up the window to separate them then the car drove off with another air force man at the wheel.

***

Six weeks later Hank was busy in the back of his shop seated at the workbench peering at Mr. Wilson's broken lawn mover engine when the front door bell chimed signalling someone had just entered the shop.

He stepped to the front to find Major Kenyon standing at the counter. Gabby Williams was noticeably absent. Kenyon appeared upset and embarrassed.

"What can I do for ya, Major?" said Hank.

"We lost it," he said his voice barely above a whisper.

"Lost what?"

"IT." He lowered his voice. "You know it." Kenyon gave him a knowing look with dark eyebrows raised over watery red-rimmed eyes. Hank discerned from the rumpled condition of his uniform Kenyon must've slept in his, for more than one night. There had to be at last two days growth of black stubble adorning his chiselled jaw.

Hank shook his head in sympathy then said, "I guess you boys blew it, didn't ya?"

Kenyon's face became red and his eyes reflected a sudden burst of anger. "It took Williams with it," he said between gritted teeth

Hank's smile disappeared and he frowned. "Well, then that's very different. I guess I better get 'im back for ya."

"How're you going to do that?"

"They don't call me the Incredible Mr. Fix-it because it's a good advertising slogan ya know." Hank moved around the counter and put an arm across Kenyon's broad shoulders as he led him to the front door. He opened the door.

"You just run along to your base and leave everything to me. I find that young fella for ya."

The bewildered major gazed at the tinker and after straightening his tie, which was askew, he marched off to the nondescript blue air force car that sat waiting to take him back to the base.

Hank watched the car until it disappeared behind a stand of trees at the end of the road where it curved. He turned and sighed heavily. Poor Gabby, a victim of his own success. Now he had to get him back. He knew the aliens were gonna be none too pleased.

He closed the door, turned to sign around to the closed side, then walked into the storage room in the back of the tinker shop. He closed the door with a thump behind him.

He walked past the shelves piled high with boxes of law mower, toaster, microwave and television parts until he'd made his way to the far wall at the back. There against the wall were three steel shelving units filled with cardboard boxes stacked to the ceiling. The boxes were labelled 'SPACE SHIP PARTS'.

Hank stared at the mountain of boxes and shrugged. Might as well get started, the sooner I start the sooner it'll be done.

The Legend of G
and The Dragonettes

I<small>T'S GOOD TO BE THE PRINCESS</small>.

Cinnamon's thoughts were interrupted when the sixty-thousand unruly, unwashed peasants in the overflowing stadium, cheered the death of latest in a long and undistinguished list of pretenders for her hand in marriage. Far below the royal platform in the arena Val the Valiant has just lost his head upon the closing of the dragon's jaw

Cinnamon sighed. Another one bites the dust. Not much a hero if you ask me.

Princess Cinnamon glanced over her left shoulder at her beloved

Dragonettes dressed in their red cheerleader uniforms and matching sneakers provided by their team sponsor, Castle Mart.

As team captain, these fresh faced girls were her pride and joy, her reason for living, except…why is there always an except?

Her intelligent indigo eyes settled on the latest in a long tradition of sworn enemies, Penny Trueheart.

Not that Penny knew she was the enemy. But such is the lot of the rival. It seemed every year someone in Cinnamon's cheerleader squad had at least one rivalry. This year it was her turn to have a rival and Penny was the rival du jour.

You're not getting my man, witc —

The smell of Val's blood wafted up and over the cheering crowd. Cinnamon was forced to cover her delicate ears as the crowd roared its approval. When sixty thousand spectators cheer you feel it as much as you hear it.

If only it had been Penny in the arena, now that would be something worth watching. But, Cinnamon had no time today to dream about the fate of Penny Trueheart. It was show time.

Her lips curled into her best look-at-me-I'm-so-pretty smile.

Behind her stood the mostly hand picked squad, with the exception of Penny, who was chosen by Cinnamon's stepmother, Queen Pepper. Cinnamon was certain the Queen had picked Penny out of spite. As you'd expect her father sided with the Queen.

The Dragonettes included; the ultra-athletic Thyme, sweet but simple Rosemary, cute-as-a-button Sage, and the twins, Garlic and Onions (pronounced O-ny-uns by Garlic and Onions rather odd parents. Garlic on the other hand, while a pungent name, is pronounced in the usual way).

Cinnamon spun round to face her Dragonettes, her pom-pom's held high, her feet set apart in the perfect position, just as they had practiced, ready to deliver the new cheer Cinnamon had written and choreographed personally.

"What do we say, Dragonettes?!"

The well-drilled unit of teenage faces beamed with youthful pride. "The Dragonettes say; Go! Dragon Joe! Go!"

Cinnamon sprang off the ground her long, not too muscular legs folded underneath her as she became airborne. She unfurled her legs and landed once more on the heavy timbers that made up the deck. She landed with a soft thump. As leader Cinnamon shook her pom-poms to signal the next sequence.

The Dragonettes yelled with wild whoops and high spirits and shouts of "Go Team!" They leaped about in what looked to the uneducated like random chaos. Of course, Cinnamon was an expert in cheerleading. Her late mother had taught her many of the finer points of cheerleading and was considered the expert in the kingdom.

The Dragonettes cheers stirred the crowd into a frenzy of blood lust. Men, women, and children rose to their feet to scream in unison, "Go, Joe! Go! Go! Go, Joe!"

Joe curled his long spiked tail and roared, his voice echoed over the crowd. As one they roared back. Joe then threw his head back and shot a river of flame high into the air. Even from the royal platform Cinnamon could feel the heat from Joe's fire.

The three hundred guards that ringed the arena had their crossbows trained on Joe in case he strayed from the script.

Cinnamon turned to face the crowd and shook her pom-pom's at the audience. This caused even more wild jubilation and wild cheers to erupt. Pagania was going to be a wild kingdom tonight.

The dragon, one of those wingless wonders, with a razor sharp bone ridge that ran up the long snout, and green scales, that were the color of mold on month old bread, covered its lizard-like body, redirected the stream of molten fire over the torso that had once been attached to Val's head. Upon contact Val's torso burst into flame, black smoke rolled outward to fill the stadium air. It overpowered the smell of Val's blood.

Cinnamon's spirit soared; the barbecued Val-the-not-so-Valiant would never become her betrothed.

Though I sure do love good barbecue, thought Cinnamon.

There would be no husband for her today. And no deflowering. The King's proclamation said that only a hero who defeated the dragon in combat had the right to claim her hand in marriage.

A barbaric rule if you ask me.

The crowd roared their approval as the hungry flames consumed the body of the late Val.

But celebration soon turned into disappointment that the end had arrived. The atmosphere of blood lust and excitement deflated as The Orator of the Games walked out from behind a wall to stand on the royal platform looking over the crowd.

The platform was in front of the royal box, where her mother and father sat on their gilded thrones, and where Cinnamon and the Dragonettes performed their routines.

The Orator, rail thin Larry the Loud, dressed in his royal blue robe with the gold thread ankle length robe, held his arms out from his sides, palms down, to signal the crowd for silence. His strong chin, with its close-cropped goatee, stuck out in the confident manner Larry always used when he performed before an audience. As one and according to an unwritten program the over stimulated crowd fell silent.

The oval shaped stadium was designed to relay the sounds in such a way that the Orator could be heard from every seat.

As Larry began to speak his baritone voice carried over the crowd. "Citizens of Pagania. Your great and glorious, King Salt has given you today the spectacle of the last challenger from the far off mysterious lands of the East. Today —"

Cinnamon tuned out the rest of Larry's speech, preferring instead to study the crowd. She felt a deep longing within her as she scanned the faces.

Surely somewhere in the world there had to be her hero, her champion.

Not that she wanted a husband necessarily, but daddy would be so disappointed if she didn't some day produce an heir and a spare. Maybe she'd even find her true love. A man who loved her that she could truly love would certainly the icing on the cupcake.

A liberated woman living in the thirteenth century who finds true love is a not as common as you might think. Even when she's a member of the thin and rich. Good thing daddy's loaded or I'd have to settle for a goat herder.

It's good to have a king for a daddy.

Cinnamon shifted her attention to the arena floor where the Dragon wranglers were herding the dragon out the massive blue steel doors located at the south end of the arena. To do this sixteen men used ten foot long poles, tipped with jagged steel spikes. It was a wise man who said I wouldn't touch a dragon with a ten-foot pole.

The dragon wranglers were the very poor who needed a job. One man is always assigned as the wrangler jester. Wrangler jesters amused the crowd by taunting the dragon as it was being taken away.

Jokes on you if he gets mad.

But the dragon didn't seem interested in the jester or the sixteen herders. His head hung low, he looked tired.

The heavy steel doors clanged shut as they closed behind them. The dragon would be locked in a reinforced iron cage deep in the bowels of the stadium, far below the arena floor.

With the death of the last hero from the East Cinnamon knew it was decision time. Larry and daddy had scoured the world to find her champion and so far they had failed to find the right man. Cinnamon decided she must take the dragon by the tail. It was time for action.

***

After she'd dismissed her team for the day Cinnamon made her way to the entry of the tunnels that ran in a spiral pattern beneath the ancient stone structure. No one knew when these tunnels had been built. Some said they were built by Alexander the Great.

The tunnels were humid and yet cool after the afternoon heat. The air was musty and stank of the centuries old build up of mold and mildew. Cinnamon wrinkled her perfect nose as made her way along the corridor. Torches burned bright and she could detect the scent of the oil used to keep them lit.

She had been given approval to visit the lower levels by the head dragon wrangler, a seedy character named Lupe.

Guys loopy alright.

There was a curve to the right in the wall ahead. She froze when she heard the heavy breathing for the first time. Though she was warm enough her lean framed trembled.

She edged around the wall, her back against cool stone. Her cheerleader uniform would need a good cleaning after this but right now she didn't care.

There it was, the dragon lying on its belly in it's barred enclosure, its eye slits closed, its thick body rose and fell in time with its breathing. Fortunately for her the bars were thick and strong enough to prevent the massive creature from swallowing her without so much as a dash of seasoning.

"I'm not an it!"

Did I say that out loud? Hey, wait a minute… did it say something?

"I said, I'm not an it!"

It spoke! "What magic is this, dragon!" she said, her voice trembled, not with bravado but with absolute terror.

"Humans. Females. Cheerleaders! Bah! Go away, cheerleader," said the dragon in his growl-speak.

Very few people these days spoke dragon anymore, but she had taken a course on dead languages at the nunnery and was fluent. The old Nun who ran the place was an expert and an excellent instructor.

"Your name is Joe, is it not?" said Cinnamon regaining some measure of confidence.

"It is." The Dragon named Joe lifted his head. His black eyes stared at her. "I should kill you where you stand," he said in a matter of fact that sent a chill through her. His eyes narrowed.

She could smell the oil and brimstone coming from the dragon's mouth as he spoke.

"I have a proposition, Joe" she said.

"A deal?" said the Dragon.

"Yes."

"Well, out with it, cheerleader. I haven't got all day. And don't get so familiar. Dragon's hate to be taken lightly. I could just as easily smoke you where you stand."

"Places to go, people to see, huh? Is that it, Joe?" She knew she was pushing, but dragons were legendary for their love of the deal.

The dragon sat silent for several seconds. Cinnamon was sure he was about to breath fire and end her world when Joe spoke again. "Come closer." Cinnamon hesitated. "Oh, don't be silly. I'm not going to barbecue you!"

Cinnamon edged forward until she stood next the steel bars that separated them. The dragon's breath was horrid. It reeked of rotten meat and decay. She managed to hold her gag reflex in check.

"I was wondering if you know of any heroes. You know…strays…who my father may have missed."

The dragon looked thoughtful then he said, "Yes, I believe I know of one. He's from some place called Houston."

"Houston? Never heard of it."

"It's very far away. But I heard about him through the dragon network —"

"Dragon network? What's that?"

Joe's eyes narrowed. "Never interrupt a dragon when they're talking," he growled his voice edged with menace.

It felt weird enough to be talking to a dragon in the first place, but a rude dragon? That was another matter.

She'd scoffed at the old Nun when they told her she'd use the dragon's language some day, but now here she was being scolded by one. Cinnamon nodded. She needed this creatures help so heap on the abuse you big, ugly lizard, she could take it.

"Before we go on," said the dragon, "let's get something straight. I'm not a creature, or a dragon for that matter. My name is Joe. I'd prefer if we stick to first names. What's your name?"

"Uhhh...do you read minds?"

"What geniuses these humans be." The dragon rolled his eyes and snorted a small ball of fire. "All I'm asking is your name, girl."

"Cinnamon."

"Like the spice?"

"Uhhh...yeah...I guess so."

"And your friend's names are Thyme, Rosemary, Sage, Garlic and Onions?" He pronounced it Onions not O-ny-uns, but she wasn't about to correct him. "What are you the spice girls?"

"Uhhh...no...we're the Dragonettes."

Joe threw his massive head back and erupted in laughter sending chills through her.

***

Cinnamon left the tunnels behind feeling the best she had in weeks. The deal was done. Joe had agreed to help her become head cheerleader. In return she'd ensure he was freed from his present job. The dragon was pleased about his freedom after she ordered the guard to release him. The guard opened his mouth to protest until she reminded him she is the princess and must be obeyed under pain of death.

It's good to be the princess.

She rounded the corner at end of the path leading to the castle and nearly bumped into Penny. Penny bowed her head when she realized who it was she'd almost collided with. Cinnamon detected Penny's jasmine perfume and felt a twinge of jealousy.

I probably reek of ode de dungeon.

"Sorry, Princess," said the pretty, petite blue-eyed blonde.

"Ah, Penny just the…I was looking for." Penny lifted her gaze a puzzled look in her eyes. "I'm planning to meet a new suitor at the edge of the village when he arrives tomorrow."

Penny's pale eyebrows rose up her forehead. "Really, Princess? Another suitor? I thought —"

"As did I until I learned of another hero. A saintly man named G."

"G? Just G?"

"No, of course not. His full name's Sir George of Houston, but he prefers to go by G. I'm told all the popular crown heads go by single letters these days. And you know how fads are; here today, gone tomorrow." Cinnamon laughed. "In a month or two he may go by Eorge."

Penny looked thoroughly confused, but she nodded anyway.

"Meet me near the end of the road, where the last of the peasant cottages are, at noon to meet this new hero. I'll introduce you. Be precise. I hear this new hero is quite punctual." Penny nodded then went around Cinnamon and disappeared around the corner.

Soon, Penny Trueheart. Soon, thought Cinnamon as she watched her rival leave.

***

Cinnamon arrived a few minutes early, which gave her time to check the thick bushes behind the row of shabby cottages. Sure enough, Joe was hidden there just as they'd agreed. Upon seeing her he gave her a wicked grin and winked. She shuddered.

I'm in league with the devil for sure. Good thing I'm a pagan.

Cinnamon left Joe in the bushes and walked back to stand beside the dirt road.

An old woman sat on a stool outside the last cottage. She seemed oddly familiar, but Cinnamon dismissed the thought. She was like any other peasant. Pathetic and poor. Between her dry lips the old woman clasped a corncob pipe. A trail of thin white smoke drifted into the air from the bowl. The woman studied Cinnamon from where she sat. Cinnamon tried to ignore the woman's gaze by looking up and down the road.

"What ya up to, Princess?" said the woman.

"You know who I am?"

"Of course," said the woman with a glint in her dark eyes. "You're one of them Dragonettes." The scent of the smoke from her pipe was pleasant it had a sweet, nutty aroma.

Cinnamon nodded. It felt good to be recognized. She'd become a celebrity. Another dream realized.

""You made a deal with Joe, didn't ya?" said the old woman. She smiled.

"How did you know?"

"I did the same thing once. I speaks their language."

Cinnamon scoffed. She speaks dragon? I hardly think so.

"What could an old woman like you gain from a deal with Joe the dragon?"

"True love. Same as you."

Cinnamon started. A chill ran up her spine. "And?"

The woman shrugged. "Turned out not too bad."

Cinnamon balled her hands on her hips. "I'm a princess. Things always turn out well for me." Cinnamon puffed out her chest and smiled. "I'm the spoiled pagan princess."

The woman cackled, as old women are wont to do, then said, "Of course, Princess. Of course." She rose from her stool and disappeared through the cottage door.

Fine way for the old lady to talk. She'd put the old bag in her place. Cinnamon placed her right thumb on her chest. "I'm the princess around here. You think I've never made a deal with a dragon before?" Of course she hadn't, but the peasant woman didn't need to know that. "Well I have, old crone. You better believe it."

Penny soon appeared in the distance coming from the direction of the castle. Once outside the thatched house of the old crone she smiled shyly at Cinnamon, which made Cinnamon wince.

Girl, you're as sweet as honey. And I hate honey.

Beyond the village, green fields lay as far as the eye could see. Against this backdrop he came. A young man, with long dark hair, broad shoulders and lean hips astride a magnificent pure white stallion. What a man, Cinnamon thought.

He wore a hat the color of new snow. It shape was unlike anything Cinnamon had ever seen. And his pure white pants, shirt, boots and saddle gave him the appearance of a white knight. His features were equal parts rugged and sensitive. His face was tanned, with a dimple on his chin. His body looked toned but not too muscular.

Cinnamon felt a strong urge to fall into his arms. He could be the one.

The old woman sat on a nearby by tree stump watching puffing on her pipe. Cinnamon could have told her to leave, but the old lady might learn something about her princess today. Fear of your local monarchy was healthy and natural.

He rode up to the two women and reined his horse as he came to a stop in front of them. The horse was a magnificent stallion that stood still and calm as could be.

"Howdy, ma'am," he nodded and tipped the front brim of his hat with the strong fingers of his right hand. Cinnamon didn't know if all the men of this Kingdom of Houston were like him, but if G was a representative sample then Huston must be one beautiful realm.

Cinnamon and Penny curtsied together. "Good day, Sir G."

"Name's plain old George. Folks jus' call me G. My daddy's name is Big G."

"Is his name George too?" asked Penny. Cinnamon glared at her. Penny looked embarrassed and averted her eyes from her leader's gaze.

"Yes, ma'am. George Senior is muh daddy's name."

"Ignore her, G," said Cinnamon. "I hope she hasn't given you the wrong impression. We don't usually ask such personal questions of strangers who come to our town for the first time."

G shook his head. "No worries, ma'am." He dismounted and stepped to the front of the horse the reins held in his right hand. "I understand thuh reason 'm here is ta slays a dragon and save a fair maiden. Is that right?"

Cinnamon nodded. "Yes, that's right."

"Well then ya'll lead me ta the arena. I gots some dragon blood ta spill."

"Actually you won't be fighting the dragon in the arena."

He frowned and she felt her go flutter. Soooo handsome. Maybe being a liberated woman in the thirteenth century wasn't all it was cracked up to be.

"Sorry, ma'am I don't rightly understand. The dragon needs ta be emulated…uhhh…I mean emasculated…I mean…"

Cinnamon couldn't hold back any more. She stepped toward G and threw her arms round his neck. G cried out in horror, ripped her arms from his neck, and pushed her away.

"What's the matter with ya'll? Women don't touch a man like that lessen they's married."

Cinnamon flushed with embarrassment, and a little anger, but she had no regret for having made her move. Secretly she had hoped to encourage him to go farther. But it appeared he was as old fashioned and stuffy as her father.

I hate rules.

Branches crunched from the row of thick bushes behind them, this was accompanied by a thump of heavy footsteps.

Joe appeared from the bushes, his scales covered in leaves, stuck there by spider's webs that now surrounded his body in a loose cocoon of spider spit. "Never fear! Joe is here!" the dragon roared.

"The dragon!" cried G as he stepped to his white horse and withdrew a four-foot long sword from a scabbard attached to his saddle. The sword's polished blade gleamed in the sunlight.

The white cowboy knight brandished the sword using both of his strong hands to wrap round the hilt. He moved with fluid and grace as he circled the dragon warily. Doubt crossed Joe's face. He glanced at Cinnamon who shrugged.

Joe cocked his head back and shot a stream of fire at the challenger. G tumbled across the grass until he once again stood on his feet the weapon again poised for battle. He wore an arrogant smirk on his handsome features. He had managed avoid the searing death-dealing flames far too easily.

As if on a cue Joe edged toward Penny who appeared to be mesmerized by the battle.

Cinnamon's lips curled in knowing smile. This was it. This would be the end of her rival. Set up. Too late for you, Penny.

The dragon whirled his massive body and his massive jaws closed over Cinnamon. Cinnamon emitted one weak cry of surprise and then she was gone.

***

G lowered his sword to his side. With a grin on his ruddy face he sauntered walked toward Penny and wrapped his left arm around her trim waist.

"I thought she'd never leave," said Penny. She patted the old woman on the knee. Thank you, mother, for teaching me dragon speak and for helping me realize my dreams." The old woman said nothing but she wore a satisfied smile on her lips.

She turned to look at Joe. "And thank you, Joe."

The dragon shrugged. "A deals a deal." Joe cocked his head. "Are you going to be the new head cheerleader of the Dragonettes?"

Penny nodded then turned to face G whose handsome features broke into a wide smile.

"Be on your way. As agreed in our double double cross deal you're a free dragon," Penny said before she kissed G hard on the lips.

The King would wonder what happened to one of his eighteen daughters, but everyone knew Cinnamon was far from his favorite. There were plenty more where she came from.

Joe disappeared into the rolling grass covered hills. eHe was never seen again. Penny Trueheart and G lived happily ever after.

And the Dragonettes? They won the regional finals and went on to become the national champions.

About the Author

International selling author, Russ Crossley, writes romance under the name R.G. Hart, mystery/suspense under the name R.G. Crossley, and science fiction and fantasy under his own. This year there will be re-issues the romantic comedies, Bachelorette: Zombie Edition by Champagne Books, and Antique Virgin by 53rd Street Publishing, a new paranormal romantic comedy, Zomopolis, and a new western romance entitled, The Fire In Their Hearts co-authored with R.S. Meger will be published in 2013 by Champagne Books. Also, look for another Aloha adventure, Bloody Betty Queen of the Pirates coming in the spring of 2013 from Champagne Books.

In addition the near future suspense novel, The Last Serial Killer by R.G. Crossley was recently released by 53rd Street Publishing in ebook and trade paperback versions.

He has sold several short stories that have appeared in anthologies from Pocket Books, St. Martins Press, at Smashwords, Amazon, and other e-retail sites.

With his wife, romance author R.S. Meger, he owns and operates a small press publishing company, 53rd Street Publishing.

The company began in April 2011 and now has over one hundred e-book titles and a number of print titles, with more planned in 2012 and 2013.

He is a member of SF Canada and the Greater Vancouver Chapter of Romance Writers of America. He is also an alumni of the Oregon Coast Professional Fiction Writers Master Class taught by award winning author/editors, Kristine Katherine Rusch and Dean Wesley Smith.

To find a complete listing of his work check out his website http://www.rghart.com, http://russstory.blogspot.com.Razor's blog can be found at http://razorandedge.blogspot.com

Feel free to contact him on Facebook or Twitter. He loves to hear from readers

Other books by the Author

Robine's Diary
The Christmas Club
Loose Ends
Splatter Pattern
It Takes Two

Anthologies
The Adventures of Razor and Edge:
Five Tales From The Quirky Detective Team

Novels
A Bad Case of Loyalty
The Last Serial Killer
Shear Murder

Titles as Russ Crossley

Novels
Attack of the Lushites
Revenge of the Lushites (coming soon)

Short Stories
Countdown
Shoeless Moe
Round Up At The Burger Bar:
The Story of Trixie Pug, Parts 1, 2, 3, 4, 5, 6, 7
Five Minutes
Blossom Queen, Barbarian
The Secret
The Family Line
End of the Flies
With Death You Get the Eggroll

The Penguin Sleeps With The Fishes
Only The Worthy
Hero For A Day
End of Empire
Strange Bedfellows
Big Business
A Perfect Crime
The Wise Guy and The Pirates
In Search of the Perfect Cup
T.I.N. Men
The Legend of G and the Dragonettes
The Incredible Mr. Fix-It
Lock Stock and Barrel
Divided Loyalties
Cave of Wonders
A Family Empire
Until We Meet Again
Dragon Rising

Presents Anthology Series
Five Tales of Urban Fantasy
Five Tales of Bizarre Detectives
Tales of Mystery and Suspense
Five Tales of Weird Fantasy
Spies, Detectives, & Heroes
Tales of Twisted Crime
Tales of The Unexpected
Tales From Space
10 by Russ Crossley
Round Up At The Burger Bar: The Story of Trixie Pug,
Parts 1- 5 The Beginning
Worlds of Science Fiction and Fantasy

More Tales of Mystery and Suspense
Ladies of the Jolly Roger
Justice Served

Titles as R.G. Hart

Short Stories
Tikka's Big Day
"My Partner the Zombie" —
Hungry For Your Love Anthology
(St. Martin's Press)
Big Hairy Deal
One Red Shoe
A Bad Day in Lunden Texas
Hook Island
Grind Manor
Bloody Betty, Queen of the Pirates (coming soon from
Champagne Books)

Novels
Bachelorette: Zombie Edition
(from Champagne Books)
Antique Virgin
The Fire In Their Hearts
with R.S. Meger (coming soon from Champagne
Books)
Zomopolis

www.ingramcontent.com/pod-product-compliance
Lightning Source LLC
Chambersburg PA
CBHW021054130626
46552CB00005B/2098